BLAST FOR ME 2

AN EYE FOR AN EYE

GHOST

Ghost

Lock Down Publications and

Ca$h Presents

BLAST FOR ME 2:

AN EYE FOR AN EYE

A Novel by GHOST

Blast For Me 2

Lock Down Publications
P.O. Box 870494
Mesquite, Tx 75187

Visit our website

www.lockdownpublications.com

Lock Down Publications
Like our page on Facebook: Lock Down
Publications @

www.facebook.com/lockdownpublications.ldp

Cover design and layout by: **Dynasty Cover Me**
Book interior design by: **Shawn Walker**
Edited by: Kiera Northington

Ghost

Stay Connected with Us!

Text **LOCKDOWN** to 22828 to stay up-to-date
with new releases, sneak peeks, contests and more…

Submission Guidelines:

Submit the first three chapters of your completed manuscript to ldpsubmissions@gmail.com, subject line: Your book's title. The manuscript must be in a .doc file and sent as an attachment. The document should be in Times New Roman, double-spaced and in size 12 font. Also, provide your synopsis and full contact information. If sending multiple submissions, they must each be in a separate email.

Have a story but no way to send it electronically? You can still submit to LDP/Ca$h Presents. Send in the first three chapters, written or typed, of your completed manuscript to:

LDP: Submissions Dept
Po Box 870494
Mesquite, Tx 75187

DO NOT send original manuscript. Must be a duplicate.

Provide your synopsis and a cover letter containing your full contact information.

Thanks for considering LDP and Ca$h Presents.

Ghost

Chapter 1

J.T.

"I ain't playing no muthafuckin' games wit you, ma nigga. This shit here is serious business," I said, as I finished duct taping the last bitch nigga to the chair.

Me and Rip had waited until the cocaine party was damn near finished, before Veronica buzzed us into the gate. With ski masks, we bussed through the pool house door with guns out. There was only four men left at the round glass table and they were taking turns, snorting up healthy lines of powdered cocaine from what seemed like two kilos on the table.

Kelly and Boris were two of the four men. One was her brother and the other, her fiancé. She had already said she didn't want either one of them killed, unless I really had to. Due to the fact that Kelly had been beefing with my cousin ever since we were kids, I was hoping I would have to knock his head off.

As soon as we bussed through the glass door with a loud *wham,* glass went flying everywhere. The doors were so weak, the one kick damn near had them hanging on by the hinges. I ran right over to the table and grabbed Boris by his ponytail, yanking him from the seat roughly, with my MAK-90 pressed so hard into his temple, it broke the skin. "Muthafucka, you gone take me upstairs to the safe and you gone empty it out or I'm gone splatter your brains all on these marbled floors," I hissed through clenched teeth.

He threw his arms into the air. His face was covered with the powdered cocaine. It looked like he'd been eating powdered donuts face-first all day long. "Listen, man, you're making a really huge mistake.

You'll never get away with this. I'd advise you to go out the way you came, and I'll forget this ever happened," he said, scrunching up his face with hatred.

Rip went up to the table and smacked Kelly so hard with his Calico gun, he fell backward out of the chair and crashed to the floor. At the same time, he pointed a MAK-11 at the other two remaining men. "Everybody, get on the ground and lay on yo muthafuckin' faces! Now!"

Kelly slowly turned over to follow his directives. His face was covered in blood and mucous. "You mafuckas will never get away with this. You're committin' suicide. Both of you."

The other two older men laid on their stomachs without a word. I sensed they were hip to the game and all they cared about was escaping with their lives intact. Both were well-dressed in expensive Gucci linens. I figured they had to have been some kind of power players in Boris' grand scheme of things.

I watched Rip grab Kelly up, then put his hand around his neck until he walked him backward and slammed him into the wall hard. "You bitch-ass nigga! You always got something to say, like you the hardest nigga in the world. Before it's all said and done, I'mma punch your brains outta yo skull, Cuz."

Boris jerked his head. "Let my hair go, you son of a bitch! If you really want to commit suicide like this, then who am I to stop you? You want the fuckin' money? I'll get you your fuckin' money! Take me upstairs, but let my hair go!" Once again, he tried to jerk his head away from me.

In one swift motion, I picked him up and then dumped him on his head. He hit the marbled floor hard. Then I knelt down and grabbed a fistful of his hair and put my face right next to his. "I don't give a fuck how bad you think you is, white boy, don't none of that shit fly wit me. Now, you gone get yo punk ass up and we gone go get this money. You make one more demand and I'm gone turn your Greek ass into a gyro! You understandin' me right now?"

He gave me a look that said he wanted to kill me in cold blood. His eyelids lowered into slits, and then he curled his upper lip. "Yez, I hear you loud and clear. Let me show you where everything is." He started to climb to his feet.

I yanked him upward and wrapped my arm around his throat from the back, putting the MAK-90 to the back of his head, ready to pull the trigger if I had to. I didn't give a fuck about him or nobody else in that house, and that included my cousin to a certain extent. My mindset was on getting every piece of money in that house, and then bouncing back to my girls. I was worried about them, and hoped they were able to handle their mission the right ski mask way. I had faith in them, but that didn't stop me from second-guessing everything. I felt like a father that had given his child the keys to his whip for the first time. Even though you knew they were ready to drive, you still worried about them every single second that car was not in the driveway.

Boris led me up the spiral staircase Veronica had already described to me. I knew once we got to the top landing, we were supposed to go straight down the long hallway, until we came to the master bedroom door. She said it was a double door that opened inward. I was waiting for him to try and take me to any other room in the upstairs part of the mansion, and I was gone make him pay for it. But, he didn't. He led me all the way to the door and opened it.

The first thing I saw was a big bed with Louis Vuitton blankets. The nightstands had L.V. on each one of them, and even the lampshades were custom-made in

Louis Vuitton. I figured Boris had some form of an obsession with the designer, because I had seen a lot of Louis Vuitton all over the house. Even looking out of the bedroom window, I could see straight downward into the big pool in the backyard. That water was clear and blue as mouthwash. Directly at the bottom of the pool, I could see the initials, L.V.

When we got into the room, I slung Boris into it roughly and he fell on the floor, looking up to me. I kept my weapon aimed at him while I went to the right-side night table and knocked it over and kicked it out of the way. I knew the safe was supposed to be under it, after you peeled the carpet back.

"Aiight, nigga, pull that carpet back and pull that mafucka up. I ain't got no time for these games. Go!" I said, grabbing his hair and pulling him in the direction of where the safe was supposed to be located.

He fell onto his stomach, and then crawled the rest of the way. He peeled back the carpet, crawling backward until I saw a digital green face light up, and buttons on the side of the screen. It looked almost like an ATM machine. He reached to press the buttons, and then stopped. "Before I do this, how do you know so much about me?" he frowned. "You come into my home and you manhandle me and my friends. Then, you come in here, knowing exactly where my safe is, as if somebody has given you blueprints on me. Tell me who it is and fuck this robbery. I'll make you a very rich man." He gave me a look that said he was serious.

I leaned down and backhanded him so hard that he flew against the side of the bed. Then I snatched him up by his hair and yanked his head backward, nearly snapping his neck. "Open that safe right now or I'm gone kill you," I growled, slinging him back on top of it.

I held the gun to the back of his head. He started to punch in the code, mumbling under his breath. Every time he punched one of the buttons, they beeped. Finally, the beeping stopped, and he took his hand and placed it on the screen. The screen went from black to all green and it started to flash for about three seconds. "System disarmed." *Beep, beep cussshhh!* The large face of the safe popped open. It was the size of a mini refrigerator.

As soon as it did, he opened the door all the way, and all I could see was stacks and stacks of money, stuffed inside of it. Grabbing him by his ponytail, I dragged him away from the safe and wrapped my arm around his neck. We fell to the floor with me squeezing underneath his jawbone with all of my might. Putting him into the sleeper hold, applying massive pressure to his jaw and chin, I could hear the bones popping in them.

He struggled against me at first, trying to slap at my forearm and twist his body this way and that way. But, there was nothing he could do, because I refused to let him go until he laid before me limp. I slammed my fist into his stomach, knocking the wind out of him and tightened my hold until he quit moving. I held it a full minute longer and then released him.

I got up and fucked up the neatly-made bed. Taking two of the pillows, dumping them out of their pillowcases, I took the pillowcases and filling them with stack after stack of money. I packed them so fast that I was sweating profusely under my hot ass ski mask. With every stack I put into the pillowcase, the smile on my face grew wider. I got to thinking about how me, Lil' Momma, and Jennifer would be able to flee to Miami, living comfortably for a minute.

I would have my mother snatched up and placed in rehab as soon as I figured out that situation. I could only imagine the pigs were going crazy looking for us out in California, which meant that we had to travel as far East as possible. I was even thinking about leaving the country altogether, because it would only be a matter of time before we were tracked down some kind of way. Them people didn't play about murders or a mafucka trying to hurt they officers. Because of Looney and the shit with him, me and the girls were on the run for both offenses.

After I emptied the safe, I ran out of the room and down the spiral staircase. I went right back into the den where I had left Rip and the other three men. What I saw made me freeze in my tracks. Rip had the two older men face down on the marbled floor with a pool of blood under them. I could see their throats had been cut wide open. The closer I got to them, the more I could make out the sadistic scene. It looked like both men's necks were open mouths. All I could do was shake my head.

Rip was just finishing up duct taping Kelly to a chair. He got up when he saw me, reached and smacked the shit out of Kelly. I could hear him screaming through the tape. "I gotta kill this nigga, Cuz. He knows who I am, and he said my name in front of them other two mafia bosses out there. Ain't no other way, but first he gone tell me where them birds at."

"Yo nigga, we gotta get a move on it though. I got the money from the safe, so body that nigga and let's bounce." I sat the filled pillowcases down. "Fuck!"

"What's good?" I noted he had a big ass hunting knife in his hand that was dripping with blood.

"I'll be back. Since you killin' everybody, I gotta go finish this mafucka upstairs, because I only put his ass to sleep. I thought we was gonna keep everything on the up and up."

He waved me off. "Hell, nawl! Go kill that nigga. Then we gotta hit Veronica's ass, because she gone flip when she finds out her punk ass brother dead, even though I don't give a fuck." Before he even finished what he was saying to me, he squished the knife through the air and sliced Kelly across one cheek. Punched him with a closed fist, then sliced him again on the other cheek. "Bitch-ass nigga, I ain't playin' wit you, you gone tell me where them birds at, so me and my people can eat, Cuz, or else it's gonna be painful until you die." He punched him repeatedly, this time so hard he fell out of the chair.

I helped him pick him back up and sit him onto it. I wanted to see exactly what he was going to do, because I never knew that he got downright mean. I thought he was strictly about that gunplay and didn't have that heinous shit in him. So, I wanted to watch every second of this. I slung the nigga back onto his chair and held him by the shoulder. Kelly was screaming behind the duct tape and I mean screaming loud. That shit had me smiling. I could only imagine how much pain he was in. I shook my head. It seemed like sooner or later, the life always caught up to bitch niggas and when it did, they rarely could handle it.

Rip took the point of the knife and poked it into Kelly's cheek and slowly broke it down his face. "Now nigga, once I take this duct tape off of your mouth, you gone tell me where them birds at. Then, you gone find some way to confirm that you tellin' me the truth, because if I detect you are lyin', then we gone have a big ass problem. You gettin' me, Cuz?"

Kelly started moving around crazy in the chair as Rip drug the knife from his mouth all the way down to his neck. Blood poured out of the wound and dripped off of his face. I could see inside of his flesh and that shit got me excited.

Rip snatched the tape off of his mouth. "Speak, nigga, and make every muthafuckin' word count."

"Ahhh!" He smacked his lips together. "It's in the wall of my manager's office at the barbershop, man. It's sixty keys of pure heroin. I swear to God, if you let me live, Rip, you can have every last one of them. And, I got one and a half million in cash put up. You can have all that shit, just let me leave out this mafucka with my life. I'm scared to die, man. Please!" He started crying like a big-ass baby and that shit made me crack up.

I smacked the shit out of him so hard, I felt my wrist snap. "Shut that bitch shit up, nigga! You down here cryin' like you ain't know what you was gettin' yoself into when you stepped into the game. Ain't no mercy, bitch nigga. None!"

There were very few things worse than a crying grown man. I hated them type of niggaz. It wasn't the first time I had pulled a caper and the nigga that got caught up started sniveling and crying like a bitch, once I started tearing into his ass. That only made me go that much harder, before I eventually killed him by drowning his ass in the bathroom toilet.

Rip stabbed the knife into his jaw. "Ahhh! Shit! Why are you doing this to me? I said I'd give you everything I got! Just stop this shit!" he hollered.

"Nigga, shut the fuck up, Cuz! I don't like all that cryin' shit either, so the more you cry like a bitch, the more pain I'm gonna inflict on yo bitch ass. You wasn't doin' alla this cryin' and shit when you were givin' the orders for yo niggaz to kill my niggaz, but now all of a sudden, big bad Kelly cryin' foul ball. Nigga, please." He pulled the knife out of his face and turned to me. "Aye, Cuz, go get Boris' bitch ass. Let me finish handling this business wit him. By the time you get back, I'll be ready."

I nodded, laughed and smacked the shit out of Kelly one more time, knocking him out of his chair. Rip stomped him in the chest and straddled him. I could hear him yelping as I jogged up the spiral staircase. I didn't want to waste no time with Boris. I was gone go right into the room, put the MAK to the back of his head and pull the trigger, knocking meat out of his taco.

We needed to get the fuck outta that house and on the road. I was already feeling some type of way because it was obvious Veronica had to be killed. I didn't trust her not to turn on me, especially after she found out that her brother had been murdered. There was no way I could sleep at night, knowing she was roaming around with all of this knowledge. I was supposed to meet up with her at Nobu at nine pm that night to fill her in on what had taken place. I planned on doing just that, but I would have Lil' Momma finish her off before the night was over with. I was sure my baby girl would have no problem doing that. That made me laugh a little bit.

I got back to the door of the master bedroom where I had left Boris and opened the door. I expected him to be lying in the middle of the floor, so imagine how I felt when I looked down and saw the spot I had left him in was empty. I felt like the entire world was closing in on me. I started to panic and wonder how long it had been since he had gotten up from that spot, and did it mean the police were on the way?

I hurried into the room and knelt down, looking under the bed, praying that he had rolled under there, even though I knew the chances of that were slim to none. My heartbeat started racing super-fast.

"Ahhhh!" *Clunk!* I felt something slam into my back. It felt like I had been hit by a school bus. *Clunk!* "You son of a bitch!" I heard Boris holler before he hit me again with whatever he had in his hands.

I fell flat on my stomach and the MAK-90 slid across the carpet. I flipped onto my back to see where the fuck Boris was, but more importantly, what he was hitting me with. I turned over just in time to see this fool with a golf club over his head, ready to bring it down again. "You black son of a bitch! I know Veronica put you up to this!"

Before he could strike me again, I kicked him directly in the nuts. I hurried to a kneeling position and tackled his ass, picking him up and crashing him into the dresser. *Boom!* The big ass mirror fell on top of us and shattered. I slung it off of me, straddled him and proceeded to punch him again and again in the face, feeling my knuckles connect with the bone in his grill. When I punched him in the nose, it broke and got stuck sideways. He hollered and kneed me in the nuts knocking me off of him.

"Get off of me, nigger!" He lunged and dived across the floor, trying to get to the MAK. His hand was almost around the handle.

Even though my nuts were in my stomach, and it felt like I was going to throw up, I bounced up and dived on top of him, right before he could get a firm grasp of the weapon. I bit into the back of his neck.

"Ahhhh! You motherfucker!" he hollered, trying to get away.

I elbowed him in the back of the head once, then punched him as hard as I could on the side of the face. Then, I jumped up and kicked the MAK closer to the door of the room, out of his reach. I hurried and grabbed the golf club and brought it down against his cranium with all of my might. *Whoom!* The driver bussed a hole right through his scope immediately. I took it and brought it down again, aiming for the same spot, because I wanted to see how wide I could get the hole. *Whoom!*

"You bitch-ass, gyro head!" *Whoom! Whoom!* I brought it down repeatedly, until his brains got to spilling out of his head. I got down on my knees and picked up my MAK-90, before jogging out of the room.

I was met by Rip in the hallway. "Look, I got this bitch nigga in the trunk. I gotta have them birds before I kill his ass. You gotta knock Veronica's head off tonight, before she finds out about all of this. I'll meet you back at the spot soon as I'm done with this nigga, Cuz."

I nodded, and ran downstairs and grabbed the pillowcase of money, before hopping into my whip and speeding to the crib. I needed to see my girls and I was missing Lil' Momma like crazy.

It took me thirty minutes to get there. When I got inside of the building, I grabbed the money and ran up the stairs two at a time until I got to our apartment door. I put the key in the lock and pushed it open, stepping in and closing the door behind me. As soon as my eyes adjusted, my heart nearly leaped out of my mouth.

I dropped the bags of money and ran over to Jennifer, wrapping my arms around her. "Jennifer, what's the matter? Where's this blood coming from? And where is Lil' Momma?"

She started crying harder, burying her face into my chest.

Chapter 2

J.T.

I dropped the bags of money, and ran over to Jennifer, wrapping my arms around her. As soon as I knelt, her arms went around me and she started crying loudly. The fact that Lil Momma was not with her already had me mentally panicking. "Jennifer, what's the matter and why is there blood all over your shirt?

"Where is Lil Momma?" I felt her nails dig into my back, as her sobs got louder. "They took her, after they shot her! They took my cousin and I don't even know what to do," she whimpered. "What are we going to do, J.T.?" By this time, she was breaking down so bad that I felt a lump form in my throat. Jennifer repositioned herself so her face was completely in my chest. Her tears had the entire front of my shirt soaked.

My thoughts were bouncing all over my brain. I felt sick, like something had happened to my best friend. I felt like I'd lost the most important person in all of my life, and I just didn't know what to do. I swallowed, as another lump formed inside my throat. My eyes were hurting, and I was on the verge of losing myself. It took all of my willpower to stand up in front of Jennifer. I knew if I broke down in front of her, she would lose it completely. So, I held her in my arms and rubbed her back. I tried to do everything I possibly could to make her feel better, even though I was panicking and damn near hysterical on the inside.

After we stayed that way for about thirty minutes, I felt it was time for me to find out what all she knew. I was beefing wit so many niggas and had hit so many licks. It could have been any one of them striking at us. I couldn't lie, my heart was extremely heavy. I missed her already. Jennifer stood up and ran her hands across her face, then shook her head wildly. Her long curly hair went everywhere. Her face was red from the hours of crying, though still beautiful. She had a scowl on it that said she was hurt and pissed off.

"They tried to kill us, J.T. Them muthafuckas, whoever they were, tried to force us off the road." She shook her head.

I was still trying to make sense of it all. "Who? What kinds of whips were they driving?" I asked, standing up and walking over to the piles of money she had on the floor. It looked like it had to be well over a hundred thousand. I couldn't even get excited about it. Lil Momma was on my mind. I had to find out where she was and who had her, or I was about to go crazy. I kept on imagining her pretty, little brown face, and that shit was making me sick. I think that's why dudes never tried to pay attention to their emotions, because we don't know how to handle them. I literally felt like I was coming down with the flu. I felt weak.

Jennifer laughed sarcastically. "They was rolling all kinds of whips, trucks, and even Ducati's. I'm telling you, J.T., they were on our ass and trying to kill both of us, and then they crashed into us, knocking us from the road. That was after Lil Momma got shot though." She broke down and fell to her knees. "I don't know if she's alive or what. The last thing I remembered was running with all of that money. We went our separate ways, because they were everywhere. Now I left my cousin behind and she could be dead somewhere, and it's all because of me. She started to break down all over again.

I dropped to my knees, and held her. "Look, you already know I'm about to get her back, even if I gotta tear up this whole city. I need for you to be strong because right now, I need the strongest version of you.

We gotta make shit happen for her, and the only way we gone be able to do that, is if we keep our heads and get on that gangsta shit. Ain't nobody finna snatch her up and live to tell about it. You already know that, right?"

I could feel her nodding her head against my chest. "Yes, but I'm still worried about her. The last time I saw her, she was leaking blood. I'm praying whoever took her had the decency to get her medical attention. I can't imagine how I'd feel if I found out that she's dead and I left her to go my own separate way. I would never be able to live with myself. I would make you kill me, J.T.," she whimpered, then began shaking as if she was coming apart at the seams.

All I could do was hold her and kiss her on the forehead as much as possible, until she calmed down enough for me to make things make sense to her, which was hard because they didn't really make sense to me. I knew she was looking to me to be her strength. For me to make everything seem as if it was okay.

I was forced to take on that role, even though inside I was losing my mind just as much as she was. You see, most women think just because a man is calm and not showing any visible emotions, it means he's not going through it. Let me tell you out the gate, that shit is not true. More often than not, we are experiencing the same emotions you are. We're just forced to handle it on the inside. I think we dwell less, but we do go through those same emotions. I was just as sick as Jennifer and I think on the inside, I was crying way harder over Lil Momma.

Boom! Boom! Boom! Boom! Somebody was beating on the door so hard, it made the hair raise up on the back of my neck. We had money all over the floor. As soon as we heard the banging, the first thing we did was scoop the money off of the floor and stuff it in a black garbage bag. After all of it was tucked away, I pulled the .44 Desert Eagle out of my waistband and put my back against the front door. "Who the fuck is it?"

Jennifer was behind me, still shaking from her emotional breakdown because of Lil Momma. A single tear trailed down her cheek, before she wiped it away and gave me a worried look. She had the big bag of money securely tied in a knot in her right hand.

Boom! Boom! Boom! Boom! The beating on the door came again. Now, I knew it had to be some bullshit. I pulled her to me and placed my lips to her ear. "Look, I know how these mafuckas get down in Vegas. If they beating on the door like this without answering you, that's only because they about to run in yo shit. So, this what I want you to do. Go in the bathroom and wait for me. We gone jump out that window and run down the alley. Mafuckas must know we hit a lick in here." I rubbed her soft face with my thumb.

She continued to look worried. "I'm not leaving your side J.T., I just can't. I need you right now and I'm not leaving you, like I did Lil Momma. Please don't make me." She bit into her bottom lip, and then it started to quiver.

I took a deep breath. "Aiight, but grab that money and take a step back, because I ain't finna play wit these niggas. Go over there," I said, pointing toward the kitchen. I didn't want her to get hit if they was gone start shooting right away. I felt like it was my job to protect her with my life, and that's what I was willing to do. I already had my mind made up that when I opened the door, I was gone start bussing. I didn't give a fuck who was on the other side. I was hip to them niggas' tricks, because it was the oldest one in the book. You keep knocking on a nigga's shit until they get irritated and answer it, then you bum rush they ass, and catch 'em off guard. It was one that I would have never used this one because to me, it was dumb. Once most mafuckas got irritated, they were ready to kill something like I was, so that's what I was about to do.

The beating started again. I clutched the pistol firm in my hand and slowly turned the lock on the door, before twisting the knob fast and falling on my back. As soon as I saw the three masked dudes, I made fire spit out of my gun.

Boo-wa! Boo-wa! Boo-wa! Boo-wa!

My first bullet slammed into the nigga closest to the door. He was wearing a black ski mask. When the bullet slammed into his face, his head jerked backward violently. He flew against the man behind him, who was also wearing the same kind of mask.

I lit his ass up too, aiming for his neck and head. One of my bullets missed and slammed into the apartment door across the hallway, after I knocked his face inward. He fell onto his side and the last nigga tried to run. I jumped up, chasing him.

As soon as he got to the stairs and damn near fell down them, I closed one eye and aimed. *Boo-wa! Boo-wa!* Both of my bullets hit him right on the top of the head. He flew into the wall, before tumbling down the stairs, and landing flat on his back. A big puddle of blood formed around him.

I jogged back to the house and stepped over the dead niggas in the doorway. Jennifer was already waiting by the bathroom door. When I got there, we prepared to jump out of the window as we heard sirens in the distance. I lowered her down until her feet touched the ground. Then, I tossed her my pistol and handed her the bag of money, before I climbed out of the window myself.

As soon as my feet hit the asphalt, we took off running down the alley. I allowed her to run in the front and I kept her pace, while I continued to look all around for predators. We saw five police cars headed in the direction of the apartment building, with their sirens blaring. My heart was really beating fast now. I got to imagining doing life in prison, and that shit spooked me worse than when I imagined how many niggas were on the other side of the door, and what they were carrying. I never feared death by the gun. I feared dying in prison. To me, that was the worst fate a man could be handed.

We ran at full speed until we got to the end of the alley that led to a busy street. Four more police cars with blaring sirens flew past, along with an ambulance. They were making so much noise, it was giving me a headache. I waited until they disappeared, and then we attempted to cross the street.

It was dark outside and looked like it was about to rain. I helped Jennifer get across and as soon as we did, she sat on the bus stop bench, and I looked around almost in panic mode. We had to get out of that area. I looked right and left, and then it started pouring rain. I mean it came down so hard, it felt like hail. Thunder roared, and lightning flashed across the sky. More police cars flew past and turned down the block of the apartment building. *Fuck, we gotta get out of this area.*

Luckily, some fat nigga pulled up to the curb in a Jeep Wrangler and got out. He had on a janitor's get-up, like he had just gotten off work. He slammed the door to his Jeep, reached and opened the back door, and pulled out an umbrella.

The rain seemed like it was attacking him out of anger. By the time he got the umbrella out, he was drenched. He opened it up with an obvious attitude, cursing to himself. Another police car rolled past with its sirens screaming. It made a right and turned· down the block the apartment building was located on. I felt like time was of the essence. The fat nigga had left the Jeep running and I was praying he was about to go into the liquor store and leave it like that, but I would have no such luck. He made it about halfway to the store's door and stopped, looked me up and down and must've thought twice about leaving his Jeep running. By this time, it was raining so hard that I could barely see in front of me. The fat man turned around and made his way back to his truck, and I knew right then what he was about to do.

I waited until he got right back to me and jumped into his path. He slightly jumped backwards and threw his guards up, like he was preparing for us to start fighting or something. I held my hands out in front of me. "Whoa, baby, I was just gone ask you if you had a cigarette I could bum. That's all, man. I don't want no trouble." Another police car turned onto our old block. Loud thunder boomed in the distance and my clothes were so wet, they were sticking to me like skin. I felt itchy under my vest and everything.

He looked me up and down and gave me a look that said if I didn't get out of his way, he was ready to kill me.

"Cuz, if you don't get the fuck out of my way asking me for a fucking cigarette, we gone have a problem." He switched the umbrella to his other hand and tilted it back some so I could clearly see his face. I noted he was missing a tooth in his upper row of teeth.

I nodded. "Aiight, homie, I don't want no problems."

I turned my back on him and walked away slowly. Jennifer held the big black garbage bag, looking around as if she were trying to locate the best escape route. I could see over her shoulder that the block was lit up with flashing lights. Once again, my panic set in. I got to imagining serving a bid and not being able to save Lil Momma, and that shit just made something in me snap.

The fat nigga mugged me for a few seconds, before stepping to his Jeep and opening the door. I waited until he got that mafucka open and rushed him at full speed, taking the back of his head and pushing forward with all of my might, slamming his face through the passenger's window. It shattered loudly.

"Uhhh. Uhhh. Uhhh," he whimpered with a face full of blood.

I punched him in the kidney and he buckled to his left knee. I slammed his face into the body of the Jeep, knocking him out cold. In the distance, the thunder boomed again.

"Let's go! Hurry up!" I ordered Jennifer.

By the time she got to me, I had pushed him out of the way. He rolled into the gutter and I jumped into the Jeep and waited for her to get in. As soon as she did, I stormed off and nearly slammed into a police car coming in our direction.

I swerved in time, skidded and punched the gas. Peeking in my rearview mirror, I saw it slam on brakes, sliding a bit before hitting a U-turn, and coming directly for us.

"Fuck!" I hollered. That was the last thing that I needed.

There we were with a bag full of money, a gun, and a stolen car I had hijacked. Not to mention, the gun traced back to the murders the policemen were on their way to.

"What are we going to do?" Jennifer yelled, looking over her shoulder. She looked like she was about to freak out as I turned so hard to my right, the Jeep nearly flipped over.

I found myself on the sidewalk, flying at nearly seventy miles an hour. Behind us, the one police car had turned into two, and they were picking up speed. The rain was coming down so hard that as soon as the windshield wipers wiped the water away, it was back as if they were pointless. "Put on your seatbelt and hurry up, because I gotta do my thing. I aint finna let us go down like this. Fuck that!"

Chapter 3

Lil Momma

Whap! Looney grabbed me by my hair and smacked me so hard, I let out a scream, before falling onto my back in the bedroom. The blow hurt so bad I found myself crying like a little kid. Before I could get used to that blow, he picked me up by the hair and smacked me again.

"Punk ass bitch. I'm gone whoop yo ass for the first couple days until you fall in line around this mafucka. You belong to me now until I figure out what the fuck I wanna do wit you. Is that understood?" he asked, smacking the shit out of me again.

This time when I fell onto the floor, I scooted on my ass, tryin' to get away from him. I wasn't trying to feel them blows no more. It was nothing like being hit by a big ass man, and Looney was huge. He had to be every bit of two hundred pounds, and damn near six foot something. I was a little chick, weighing less than a hundred and twenty, so he was fucking me up and I was over that.

"Looney, why are you doing this to me?" I whined, feeling my left eye slowly close.

He knelt down as I scooted away from him, and grabbed my foot, pulling me back to him. "Bitch, because that nigga love you to death, so if I take you away from him, he'll be destroyed. He done already left you out here to fend for yourself. What type of nigga lets his bitch get shot and leave her out in the cold? You know how much it cost me to have my white nurse bitch get you right? Huh?" He raised an eyebrow and dragged me back to him, before pushing me on my back and straddling me.

Ghost

My heart started to pound in my chest right away. I was praying he wasn't about to do what I thought he was. I wasn't going to be strong enough to fight him off, but I was going to do my best. He was gone have to beat me senseless to get into my body. Though, I was pretty sure he wasn't gone have no problem with that. I felt him lean down and suck on my neck, before licking it. I felt sick immediately. "Looney, what are you doing?" I cried, especially when I felt his hand go between us and rub over my crotch. His fingers actually separated the lips through my jeans.

"I'm finna hit this pussy. That's the least that's gone happen right now. That nigga was always all up under you. It gotta be because you got some bomb-ass pussy. Well, I'm gone find out for myself. I feel like it's my right to." He sat up, ripped open my pants, and yanked them down my legs, before throwing them over his shoulder. He rubbed the front of my panties and caused them to go inside of my lips.

"Please don't do this, Looney. I ain't got nothing to do with the beef between you and J.T. Y'all are men, that's manly business," I cried.

He ripped my panties away from my body, leaned down and bit into my neck. I could feel his fingers feeling around my pussy, before two entered me, and started to move in and out swiftly. His thumb ran circles around my clitoris.

I tried to close my thighs with all of my might, but he pinched me and made them pop back open. He sat up for a moment to take his shirt off. He had so many muscles that it looked like he worked out all day, every day. His body was covered in tats. "I don't give a fuck how much you fight me, when it's all said and done, you gone give me this pussy and I'mma know what inside of you feels like."

He sped up the pace with his fingers. It felt like he added a third before pulling my blouse open, exposing my breasts, sucking on them as if he were a hungry infant. "Damn, you got some big ass nipples. Yo shit long, like you been pulling on them your whole life." He frowned and trapped one with his lips, speeding up the pace of the assault between my legs.

I ain't even gone lie and as much as I hate to admit it, all that shit he was doing was causing me to get wet. I just couldn't help it, and I was disgusted with myself. But, every time his thumb rubbed across my clit or his three fingers went deep inside of me, or I felt his tongue run circles around my nipple before pulling on them with his teeth, I felt my pussy gush out its juice. My legs involuntarily popped open as if I wanted him to do more when mentally, I wanted him to stop because I was sickened. Sexually, I was curious as to what he was going to do next.

He pulled his fingers out of me and I felt empty. He brought them to his nose and sniffed, before sucking them into his mouth hungrily. I mean, he slobbered all over them, and even licked in between his fingers. The noises he made were making me feel some type of way. "Damn, this that salty shit. You so mafucking wet right now. You ready for this dick. All I wanna hear you say is that you want me to take this pussy. That you want me to hit this shit like I'm supposed to," he growled.

"No!" I tried to push him away from me. "Don't do this. Please don't do this."

He pushed me onto my back and forced my knees to my chest, and my pussy popped out from between my legs. Before I could try and get away, his whole mouth sucked my sex into it. It sounded like he was slurping up oysters.

Chills shot up my spine and my whole body started to shake uncontrollably. His teeth nipped at my clitoris and his tongue forced its way into my hole and ran in and out of me. Before I could stop it from happening, I was coming so loud, I was embarrassed. He kept on sucking and licking until his face was covered in my juices.

"That's what I'm talking about. You can't fight this shit.

I already told you I'm finna hit this pussy. Just let go and let me do me." He flipped me on my stomach and opened my ass, taking his tongue and licking in between it, fucking me with it over and over again.

I moaned and tried to catch my breath. "Stop, Looney. Please stop doing that shit to me. I ain't got. I ain't got. Nothing. To do with you and J.T.'s beef. Please, just…" He slid his fingers back into me and started to work me over at full speed.

"I want this pussy dripping wet before I buss that mafucka open. I'm 'bout to blow yo back out." He pulled me up to my knees and slapped his long, fat dick on my ass, before trailing the head up and down my lips, searching for my hole's opening.

I felt myself shaking. It felt like he had a whole lot of meat and I was scared. Not only didn't I think I could take it, but I was worried about him hurting me on purpose. I knew he hated my man, and I just didn't want him to take that shit out on me. I was already dealing with my shoulder issue.

Looney took his dick and started to enter me. I felt myself opening wider and wider. It felt like he was trying to stuff me like a Thanksgiving turkey. He pushed my face into the floor and slammed all the way in, taking my breath away. He kept his dick all the way in me and didn't move.

"Now, by the time I'm done hitting this pussy, I'mma make you call me Daddy, that's the only way

32

I'mma pull out of you. If you don't call me that, I'mma keep on beating this shit to death. That's my word." He pulled all the way back until his head was on my lips, then he slammed back into me and started to fuck with me an attitude while he gripped my hips and smacked my ass. "Umm, shit. Umm shit!" he groaned, with my ass crashing into his lap over and over again. I could feel my juices running down my thighs, further embarrassing me. "Fuck, I knew you had that good shit! That nigga ain't sniffing around you for nothing! I'm finna kill this pussy!" he growled.

Smack! Smack! Smack! Smack! He was fucking me over, riding me from the back like I owed him money. He pushed my face into the floor again and I screamed. He was doing me wrong.

"Reach under yourself and rub that clit. Come on now! Hurry up. I need you to make this pussy wetter. Now!" he hollered, fucking me so hard, all I could do was cry into the carpet. He smacked me on the ass loudly. *Whap!*

I moaned out loud and turned my face to the side, with my eyes closed and mouth wide open. Reaching under us, I trapped my clitoris and pinched it, sending shivers throughout my body. I felt my pussy skeet. "Shit!"

"Yeah, that's what I'm talking about, bitch! I feel that shit getting wetter. Keep doing it and I'm finna come all in this pussy." He sped up the pace and started slamming into me like he was trying to go through me.

I closed my eyes and imagined him being J.T., because he got down the same way. I missed him so much, and I knew he would kill Looney for doing this to me. I imagined his rock-hard body and how much he cared about me, and it all just turned me on. I got so far away from reality, I started slamming my ass back into Looney at full speed, daring him to fuck me harder.

"You ain't doing shit! You ain't doing shit. J.T. still fuck better than you. He still my everything. He…uhhhhh-sheeeit! Oh sheeeit!" I screamed.

Looney started to really rock me. I could feel his dick get longer and then, he was coming in me. I felt the hot globs of his nut hitting my walls. Then, he pulled his dick out and started nutting all over my ass and back, while he played with my clitoris. I knew my pussy was wide open, because I could feel the air going inside me. He pushed me onto my side and picked up my thigh, before sliding back into me and fucking me hard for two hours straight. True to his word, he didn't stop until I called him Daddy. I threw up immediately afterwards.

After I finished puking, he pulled my hair back and got into my face. "I know that nigga got stupid bread now. I done heard about some of the licks he hit. In order for that nigga to get you back, I gotta have two hundred stacks. Ain't shit moving until then."

Chapter 4

Rip

I threw Kelly's punk ass on the floor and pointed my
TEC at his ass. I was ready to blow this nigga's head off.
I was tired of playing games. "Take me straight to the
safe. I ain't trying to hear shit else." I lowered my banger
and aimed for his knee. *Bop! Bop! Bop!* Three quick
bullets ripped into it, knocking it from his leg and
leaving a bloody hole that oozed his plasm.

"Ahhhh! I told you I was gone give you
everything! You ain't gotta do this shit to me! Please!
Help me! You ain't gotta do this," he cried out, with tears
rolling down his face. He looked like a straight-soft bitch
nigga. I hated when niggas cried when they found
themselves on the other end of a banger. When the tables
got turned around and they was the victim, I felt like a
mafucka should have that same "G" they had when they
was bussing at a mafucka. So, the more he screamed, the
more I wanted to punish his bitch ass.

I grabbed him by the neck and forced him to get
up. He hopped on one leg, with drool coming out of the
corners of his mouth.

"Take me to the muthafucking safe. If I gotta say
that shit again, I'm fucking you over in an ugly way." I
pushed the shit out of him and he fell flat on his stomach.

He crawled across the floor, looking over his
shoulder at me. "You can have the money, boss. This shit
ain't worth dying over. Take me to the room at the end of
the hallway right there. As soon as we enter the room, all
I gotta do is peel the carpet back, and the safe will be
right in the floor. It's digital, so all it needs is my
fingerprints, and my four-digit code."

I kicked him in the ass with the point of my foot. He had on these flimsy ass Versace pants, so he had to feel the whole point all in his shit. "Stop doing so much talking and show me what the fuck I need to see." I kicked him again, this time so hard that he stood up, before falling back down onto his stomach.

"Awright man, damn! Stop treating me like I'm a bitch! I already said I'll give you everything!" He sat on his ass and gave me a look that said he hated me. And I didn't give no fucks.

Whoom! I delivered a kick to his face causing him to flip over onto his back, knocking him out cold. Blood poured out of his nose, and the corner of his mouth was split open so wide, it looked like I'd cut him open with a steak knife. I slapped the shit out of him. "Get yo punk ass up, Cuz!"

"Uhh! Uhh!" He looked disoriented. He started to scoot backwards on his ass. By the time he looked up at me, I had my TEC-9 pointed at his forehead, ready to pull that trigger.

This bitch nigga started screaming like I was raping him. "Ahhh! Ahhh! Help me!"

Bop! Bop! Bop! I let off three shots into his right kneecap. If the nigga wanted a reason to scream like a bitch, now he had one. I reached down, grabbed the other leg and drug him across the floor, leaving a trail of blood behind us. It looked like he was leaking paint.

When we got to the room at the end of the hall, I threw him inside of it and started to peel the carpet back. It didn't take long before I saw the safe he was talking about. It had an all-red, digital-face Secure-Pro. I knew about them joints. I'd fucked over a few kingpin niggas that fucked with them boys. I laughed at that. This nigga had to be holding, because that safe cost a minimum of ten gees, and that was for the smaller kind. This mafucka

I was looking was huge. He had to have dropped some coins for it.

I grabbed him by the back of the head and threw him down in front of it. "Open that bitch, nigga, and hurry the fuck up." I put the TEC to the back of his head. I couldn't wait to splatter his shit. I hated whiny niggas.

He slowly rose into a push-up position and placed his hand on the portion of the safe that called for him to do that. After it beeped three times, a voice that sounded like Siri's said, "Please enter your four-digit security code." I saw him punch it in and it didn't do nothing for what seemed like an eternity.

I got to thinking his safe had a built-in code that automatically called for the police. I immediately got nervous.

"Yo, why it ain't doing shit?" I slammed the barrel to the back of his head.

"Ow! Chill the fuck out and give it a second." He stared at it for a little while longer and then the face started to flash brightly.

Siri's voice came back on. "Your current total is two hundred and fifty thousand dollars. Please enter the amount you will be withdrawing."

This nigga started pressing on it again, and I got to feeling like that was a stall tactic. For some reason, I just didn't trust that shit. I had a bad feeling that something wasn't right. My stomach flipped over more than once, and then something told me to look to my left and move. As soon as I did, a gun sounded.

Boo-wa! I felt the bullet fly past my face and smack into the wall to my right. I dropped to the floor as more shoots were let off. *Boo-wa! Boo-wa!* The fire lit up the dimly lit house. I saw Kelly's slick ass trying to make a clean getaway on his stomach, leaving a trail of blood.

I dropped to my knee as I saw the white man aim at me. I fired. *Bop! Bop! Bop!* That aim was on point. The bullets ripped into his chest, sending him into the air and on his back. Another white man in a suit opened the patio door and came through it with two pistols in his hands, like he was about to be on business. Before he could even get in the house good, I finger fucked my machine. *Bop! Bop! Bop! Bop!*

He flew into the air and back out through the patio door. This shit had a nigga excited. I waited for the next fuck nigga for a few more minutes. When none came, I ran over and kicked Kelly in the back so hard, I heard his shit pop.

"Arrrgh!"

I picked him up, carried him over to the safe and body slammed his ass on top of it. "Open it! Now!" *Bop! Bop! Bop!*

I fired three shots in his ass, knocking chunks of his meat away. That nigga opened the safe so fast as if his life depended on it. As soon as it was opened wide enough for me to handle my business, I grabbed him by the leg and drug him away from it. Standing over him, I smiled. "You tried that weak ass shit. Bitch nigga, I knew you had security. You too soft not to. Now, where the fuck yo sister at?" I asked.

Victoria was the bitch that had set shit up so me and my cousin, J.T. could hit up a bunch of mad men. I knew I needed to whack her ass, even if J.T. didn't. That bitch's mouth could get us in trouble and I wasn't geeing for that.

Kelly was struggling to breathe. His eyes rolled into the back of his head more than once. I could tell that he was on his way out. I needed to get as much information from him as possible before he flatlined.

I knelt beside him and stuck my thumb into the bullet hole in his knee. I dug deep into it and twisted my thumb. He screamed at the top of his lungs and tried to scoot away from me like I was killing his ass.

"Phoenix, bro. She got a house in Phoenix over on Carpenter Road. A big gray house. Twenty-three-eighteen. That's the address. I gave you everything that you asked of me. Now just leave me alone. Let me lay here and go to sleep." He turned on to his stomach and closed his eyes.

I went into his fancy ass kitchen and looked around until I found some garbage bags. As soon as I found them, I grabbed two and came back into the den where the safe was. I loaded it up with all the money and tied the bag into a knot. Then, I jogged over to him and knelt down. I took the last garbage bag and wrapped it around his head, before I sat on his back and watched him struggle underneath me until his body went limp.

I left out of there with a bag of money, and murder on my mind. I had to find Victoria, and I had to find out what was good with J.T.

Chapter 5

J.T.

Errrrr-uh! Whoorn! Tishhhh! I crashed through the department store window until the Jeep slammed into the counter, knocking the cash register off of it.

Luckily, the store was closed because had they been open, I would have killed somebody. I looked over at Jennifer. She took her seat belt off and grabbed the bag of money from the back seat.

"Let's go! We can hit it out the back door. Those two police cars that were behind us crashed about two blocks ago. Hurry up!"

I followed her as we found the back door and shot out of it. Once again, we found ourselves in an alley, running full speed. She blew my mind when she came to a fence and scaled it with no problem. I threw the money over to her and did the same thing.

We landed in somebody's backyard before running out of it, onto the side of their house, with lightning threatening to strike overhead. The rain began to fall hard, and I damn near busted my shit more than once. I didn't know how Jennifer was able to keep her balance, but she didn't have nearly as many problems as I did.

When we got to the front of the house, lightning struck.

Boom! A big ass tree fell down hard onto somebody's yard, and it caught fire. Behind it, a power line flashed blue before the whole block went pitch dark.

I had the feeling like at any moment, I was about to be struck. I felt damn near hysterical and scared as a muthafucka.

Jennifer was humping it like she didn't have a care in the world. More than once, I had to run with all of my speed just to catch up to her. She looked over her shoulder. "We gotta get a new car!" Her face was drenched in rain and her hair all over the place. She looked like a wet ass Ashanti.

Boom! Lightning struck another tree, this time it came down and crashed into somebody's house across the street. It made a noise so loud, it had my ears ringing. You talking about scared, I was out of my mind, freaking out. We ran on the side of another house and jumped the fence at the back of it, before doing it again at the next house. But, when we came to the front of this one, I saw an all-black Escalade truck. I ran right up to that bad boy and busted the back window out with the handle of my gun. It shattered and I climbed through it. Two minutes later, I was peeling away from the curb with Jennifer sitting in the passenger seat.

* * *

Lil Momma

"I don't need her to wash me up. I can do this shit on my own. I'm a grown ass woman," I said, lowering myself into the bath water J.T.'s sister, Jamie, had run for me. As soon as I slid into the water, it was like I was being relieved of so much pain and tension. I couldn't help closing my eyes. Not only was my shoulder killing me, but so was my middle. Looney had done a number on me. I was all reamed out. I needed to soak for a minute.

Looney knelt down and grabbed me by the face. He got all up in my grill. I could smell the cigarettes on his breath.

"Bitch, I don't know if that nigga, J.T., let you run shit over there when you wit him, but that shit ain't happening wit me. In my book, you a prisoner of war, and I don't negotiate wit terrorists. Now, I sent her in

42

here so she could wash you up, because that's what I ordered her to do. I run this shit. You gone lay yo ass back and let her do what the fuck she gotta do. You understand me?"

I nodded my head and he leaned in and kissed me on my lips that were pursed out like a fish. Sucking on them loudly, before pushing my head away. I felt sick on the stomach, and like I wanted to kill him.

He stood up. "Jamie, I want that pussy so clean, you should be able to eat out of it when you done. And, it better be spotless, because that's definitely what you gone do when I get back in here." He walked out and slammed the door.

Jamie dropped to her knees and grabbed the loofah, pouring body wash onto it, and dunking it under water to get it wet and soapy. "Look, I don't want no problems wit him. That nigga's crazy. You might as well let me go ahead and wash you up. That way, this part of the process can be done. I don't want him kickin' my ass on account of what you doing wrong." She took the loofah and started washing my back.

I didn't feel like arguing or fighting with her. I just wanted it all to be all over and done with. The last thing I needed was for him to kick my ass. After all, I did need a bath. I was starting to smell myself before he mentioned me getting in the tub.

Jamie was quiet the whole time she washed me up. It was like she was afraid to speak or something. I wondered if he had the bathroom hooked up some kind of way, so he could hear us.

"Hey, you're J.T.'s big sister, right?" I asked, looking her over closely. We had met a few times and I knew who she was. I just wanted her to say anything, just so I could feel her out.

She nodded her head. "Yeah, that's my little brother, although he acts like he older than me, so sometimes I be forgetting."

She dunked the loofah again, and washed across my breasts, lifting one at a time to get under them before dunking it again, and applying more body wash. "You acting like we don't know each other. I know you're my brother's heart. That nigga crazier about you than he is me." She lathered the loofah. "I need you to put your leg up on the rim of the tub, so I can get your pussy like he told me to. I wanna make sure when he sticks his nose in there, it's fresh, or he gone kick my ass." She looked down on me and gave me a look that said she wanted to be done.

I stood up and put my foot on the rim of the tub. She reached and peeled my lips apart, lathering them with soap, before sliding two fingers into me. I damn near fell backward, because that caught me off guard. She had to grab my arm or I would have bussed my shit.

"Whoa, my bad. I didn't mean to scare you. I'm just trying to make sure this smell-good get all the way up in your box. I use this and it's good for my pH-balance. It isn't harmful or anything, but you gotta get it up there." She massaged her fingers back into me, before pulling them out and sniffing.

She nodded her head. "Yeah, I gotta get you right. So how did my brother lose you?"

"Your brother didn't lose me. When all this shit happened, I wasn't with him. I was with my cousin, and he blindsided us. Had J.T. been there, he would have murked that fool. That I know for sure."

She snickered, shaking her head. "Yeah, my brother crazy. I know that for a fact. I done watched him do some things to niggas growing up that's still fucking wit me." She shook her head. "I love him though. Damn, I see you got a lil tight kitty, huh? She frowned. "That's probably why my brother so crazy about you too. That and he tell me you so stomp down. That's what's up."

Her comment about my pussy threw me all the way off. She said it like we were cool as snowballs. I felt her fingers go into me again and I slightly moved off of them. "I'll be back with him soon. After Looney get ahold of him and tell him what my ransom is, that shit is as good as paid. Trust me on that."

Jamie exhaled, and nodded. "I don't know why they hate each other so much. Deep down, I think it got something to do with me. My brother's always been jealous of any male that treated me wrong. Well I guess I shouldn't say jealous, more like hated any nigga that did me wrong before. He always been real over-protective of me."

I know she was J.T.'s sister, but hearing that had me jealous as a muthafucka. I didn't like him caring about nobody other than me. I wanted to be his everything and I felt like I earned that right. The fact that she was his sister didn't lighten my feelings toward that matter in the least bit. I missed him so much, it was killing me. I wondered if Jennifer had made it back to him safe and sound.

Looney opened the bathroom door and stepped into it. "You ready to prove to me that her pussy clean enough, Jamie?" He asked this with a handful of Jamie's hair.

I took the nozzle and sprayed it into my kitty, making sure I washed it out good. "I'm clean, Looney. She did what you asked her to do. Please don't beat her ass, I'm begging you." I looked down on Jamie· and she looked terrified, like she was scared for her life.

He smiled. "This bitch been in here giving you a bath for ten minutes and already, you begging me on her behalf. Well, ain't you just the nicest mafucka in town."

45

He yanked her head back roughly. "Eat that bitch pussy and prove yourself to me. You already know how this shit go." He threw her forward toward me.

She crawled over to me and placed her hands on both of my thighs. "Open up, Lil Momma, before he kill me. Please," she whimpered.

I was caught between not allowing that to happen and trying to rush Looney's ass. I knew niggas were naturally stronger than women, but I felt that if me and Jamie teamed up, we could whoop his ass.

I felt her trying to pry my thighs apart. "Please, Lil Momma. I don't feel like dealing with this shit tonight. Just let me prove myself to him, then I can go and cook. I already know my duties around here."

I swallowed and thought about J.T. I wondered what he would say if he knew his sister was knelt down in front of me trying to get me to allow her to do what she was asking of me.

* * *

J.T.

"Alright, that's cool. Just throw that on the floor, and get over here," I said, taking off my shirt, and unsnapping my bulletproof vest. I was itching so bad under there it felt like a million bugs were crawling all over me. I don't know why most niggas made it seem like wearing a vest was the coolest thing in the world, because it wasn't. They were hot and heavy. They made you sweat easily, and a lot. And if you needed to wear a vest, it was because you knew your life was in constant danger all day every day, so tell me what was really cool about that?

Jennifer placed the bag of money on the floor next to the complimentary bathrobes and ran over to me. I wrapped her in my arms, hugging her tightly. "We got through it, J.T. We actually got away, I was so scared." I could hear her sniffin' her snot back into her nose. I held her firmer, then leaned down and kissed her on her wet forehead. I noted we both smelled a lil funny, but I blamed that on the rain, and all of the running we had to do.

"Ma, why don't you go ahead and get in the shower first, and then I'll jump in right behind you. Once we get nice and clean, then we can focus in on other things, like how we're gonna get Lil Momma back." I rubbed her back and kissed her forehead again.

She stood on her tippy toes and my lips pressed against her skin even firmer. I could see she had her eyes closed, with a slight smile across her face. After the kiss, she took a step back and looked up at me. "You always make me feel so safe, J.T. Like, whenever I'm with you, I just know that in the end everything will be okay. I trust you with my life, and I love you so much." She crashed into me and laid her head back on my sweaty chest. My chest muscles jumped. The heat from her face made me feel warm inside. Wasn't no secret that I cared about Jennifer. She had been through a lot in life.

Alongside me and Lil Momma, I felt something deeply for her within myself. I didn't know exactly what it was because Lil Momma was my baby, my heart. But, when it came to Jennifer, it was so hard to not be crazy about her. She was so loving. So stomp down, and trusting in me. I knew off top I would knock a nigga's head off for her with no hesitation. I didn't even give a fuck if it was a nigga from my own bloodline. I had her back, and I didn't give a fuck what nobody thought about it.

I could hear her sniveling a little bit under me. "Come on, let me run this water for you, so we can get you all clean. You know you'll be feeling like a goddess once them suds do they job, Ma."

She unleashed herself from me and smiled, after wiping her tears away. Her beautiful face was all red around the eyes. Her baby hair along the edges of her temple and forehead was all curled up. "Yeah, that's probably why I feel extra low it's because I'm dirty, so let me get clean and see what that do. But, wait a minute. We don't have any clean clothes. What are we going to do?"

I hadn't even thought about that. The clothes we had on were wet as hell. I could tell they were going to get that mildew smell to them in a minute, and that would suck. "I'll tell you what, why don't you just jump on in the shower, and I'll try and figure out that part in a minute. I mean, worst come to worst, they did give us these robes. So, if we have to rock them until our clothes dry, then that's just what we'll do. The most important thing to me is us getting clean."

She nodded her head and started the shower water, leaning over with her long curly hair all over her face. I had to leave out of the bathroom, because curly hair had always done something to me as a man. Not only that, but Jennifer was fine. Light-skinned with brown eyes, she wasn't skinny, or fat. She was in between, real thick, with a little stomach. You know, a real woman for the most part. The coldest thing about her to me was the fact that she didn't even know she was so bad. Her self-esteem was lower than a midget's ankle. But, I'm telling you she was bad. So, I had to get out of that bathroom or I was gone be all over her. I did wait until she was actually in the shower with the door closed to grab her dirty underwear and clothes.

I took them to the sink in the kitchen and washed them by hand. It felt weird as hell washing out her little panties too. But, when you cared about a woman and you

wanted to be there for her by any means, you did what
you had to. So, all you niggas out there saying that's
some shit you would never do, then all you really care
about is you.

After I washed everything, I hung them by the
heater, then I stripped down to my boxers and did the
same thing with my clothes. I'd wash my underwear out
in the shower. I ain't want her to come out and see me
walking around naked. I mean, I don't think it would
have been a problem, but I just decided against it.

My phone buzzed, and I damn near broke my neck
jumping over the bed to get to it. As soon as I saw the
name on the face, I knew right away it was Looney's
bitch ass. I thought that nigga was still in the county after
we'd got into some bullshit with a few police. "What the
fuck you calling my phone for, nigga?" I spat into the
phone with so much venom, I didn't even notice I was
squeezing my phone with all my might, until I heard it
cracking. I loosened my grip.

Chapter 6

J.T.

"Whoa, bitch-ass nigga. Calm yo punk ass down before I shoot this bitch in the face and post that shit on Facebook," Looney laughed.

I felt my heart pounding in my chest. I know this nigga wasn't talking about doing something to my sister or my mother, for that matter. I knew they both were living with him at one of his cribs. I just didn't know which one. My sister was obsessed with the nigga. They had one of them relationships where he would physically put his hands on her and then she'd run to me, but when I got ready to fuck him up in my own way, she would beg me not to. Then, she would be back with him the same week. I had to wash my hands of that situation, or I would have constantly been beefing wit every Blood on the West Coast because that nigga, Looney, was plugged.

I held my tongue and waited for him to go on. The whole time I had visions of killing him in cold blood. I had hated that nigga ever since our first falling out back in the day.

I could hear him laughing. "Oh, so now you all quiet and shit. What happened to that loud mouth pussy that answered the phone?" he hollered.

"Yo, Looney, you already know how I get down, nigga. If you put a gun in my sister or my mother's face, you gone have to kill me, blood. Now, I told y'all that I would stay out of yo business, as long as y'all didn't bring me into that shit. But you purposely calling my phone on this dumb shit, so what's good, my nigga?"

Jennifer came out of the bathroom with the white robe on, looking like a Brazilian model. It was opened a little bit so I could make out a nice portion of her

Ghost

cleavage that gravity had touched just a little bit. She had
the body of a real woman. Not that fake shit you see on
TV and was supposed to believe to be real. "J.T., you
seen my clothes?" She looked nervous.

I nodded and pointed to the heater where all of her
things were drying. I saw her look over to them and
smile.

"Mother? Sister? Nigga, I ain't talking about
neither one of them. I'm talking about yo bitch, Lil
Momma!"

As soon as he said her name, I damn near dropped
the phone. He was the last person I would have thought
had her. My heart got heavy right away because I knew
that nigga, Looney, was a sicko. Depending on how long
he'd had her, it was almost a guarantee he had already
fucked her, that's just how he got down. I grew up with
the nigga and it was one of the reasons why we didn't
jam. I wasn't with raping no women, no matter how
much power I had in our organization, and that nigga
made it a sport. He was a proud rapist. "What's this
about, Looney? Why you fucking wit my people?"

Looney didn't waste no time. "I want two hundred
gees! You want this bitch back, that's what it's gone cost
you."

"Name the place. You ain't saying shit. I got that
right now for her." I was pacing around the room like I
wanted to kill something. I imagined this bitch-ass nigga
with his hands all over her and I just got heated. That
was my baby. I'd do anything for her.

"We can do this shit tomorrow. We can meet up at
Fat Burger over on Crenshaw, at three pm. You have my
money, and I'll have yo bitch, nigga. Simple as that."

"Did you touch her? Fuck nigga, did you put yo
rapist-ass hands on her?" I was so mad my vision was
getting blurry.

52

Every time I imagined this punk ass nigga forcing his self on her, I wanted to snap the fuck out.

Looney laughed. "Do you even have to ask?" He made a noise to indicate I was asking a stupid question, and it got me so heated, I didn't even know I'd pick my gun up and was pacing back and forth with it. My finger was on the trigger, squeezing. Luckily, the safety was on, or there would have been bullet holes all over that room.

"I'll be there, Looney. Just have my baby there, and I'll have yo bread."

* * *

After I came out of the shower, I could feel myself still heated. I placed my boxers next to the rest of my clothes and made my way over to the bed where Jennifer sat with her head down. I slid beside her and wrapped her into my arms. I could smell the shampoo and conditioner she'd washed her hair with.

She smelled clean and feminine. Like a woman, and that appealed to my senses. I brushed her hair out of her face. "What's the matter?"

She shrugged her shoulders. "I don't know. I guess, I just hope that we get my cousin back tomorrow. I really miss her. I know she thinks about us all the time like we do her." She snuggled into me, and the way she was laying on her side slightly, caused her robe to open enough for me to make out one full tittie. The nipple, big and brown.

I did everything I possibly could to take my mind off of what she was accidentally exposing to me, but it was so hard. And by it, I meant it. She must have felt it, because she sat up and gave me a crazy look. All I could do was lower my head, and make it seem like something was bothering me.

Jennifer took my face into her hand, rubbing it. "Are you okay, J.T.? You look like you're sick or something, but at the same time, I can feel you poking me." At saying the last part, her voice faded out. I looked into her eyes and damn, she was fine. That shit was getting the better of me. Then, on top of that, she smelled so clean. That, mixed in with the fact that I needed some pussy and was so stressed out. Before I knew it, I had her up in the air with her legs wrapped around me, tonguing her lil fine ass down, while she moaned into my mouth loudly. We attacked each other, and our breathing was labored.

While I held her in the air, I lowered the top of her robe, so I could see them pretty titties. They sagged just a little bit. Enough to make them real and so fucking sexy to me. We crashed into the door of the hotel room. I could feel her hot pussy up against my stomach. I palmed them titties and sucked one big nipple into my mouth. Twirling my tongue around it, before sucking like she owed me some milk out of it. She moaned loudly and forced my mouth to the other one, as if I was gone forget about it or something. I sucked that big nipple into my mouth and nipped at it with my teeth. Wiggling out of my robe and helped her do that same. Now I really felt her heat.

I carried her to the bed and threw her down on it, before kneeling down on the side of it and pulling her back to me.

"Open them legs, baby. Let me see that fat ass pussy. I wanna eat that mafucka."

She hissed through clenched teeth. "Ummm, okay." She opened her thick thighs wide. Took two fingers and parted her sex lips, exposing her pink center. Her womanly scent wafted into the air, and it drove me crazy. There wasn't nothing like the smell of pussy to me. I'm talking the natural scent too, not that bullshit that most females try and add to their kitties. Nall, I loved the real. The untampered with scents, that's what drove me crazy.

I stuck my face in between her legs and licked up and down her crease. Her sex lips were already slippery with her juices pouring out of her. She tasted a little salty, but not much.

I ran my thumb in circles around her vagina's nipple, and she arched her back, moaning loudly. "Jennifer, just let me attack this mafucka until you come in my mouth three times. After you come three times, then pull me up and I'mma stuff this pipe in you. You hear me?" I slurped her pussy lips into my mouth.

"Uhhhh, shit! Yesss, J.T.! J.T.! I hear you, baby!" She opened her thighs as wide as they could go, while I feasted on her lucky charms.

I licked all up and down, and in between them fat lips. I trapped her clitoris with my teeth and nipped at it, before sucking it into my mouth. When she came the first time, she started to scream and shake at the same time. I kept her clitty trapped in my lips, nipping it over and over again with my teeth.

Then, it felt like she was peeing in my mouth. Her juices were all over my face, dripping off of my chin. I kept on going, flicking her clit and sucking. When she came the second time, she popped her hips forward and grabbed my head, forcing my face into her pussy, actually riding it like it was a dick.

She squirted, and I caught it right on my tongue, swallowing.

For the third one, I flipped her on to her stomach and ate her pussy from the back. Slurping it up with her ass cheeks on my forehead. She pulled them apart, and I licked all in her ass and sucked her berry, like I was trying to take it off.

She screamed into the pillow, rose to her knees and fell back onto her stomach, shaking like crazy. I left her shaking. I took a step back and stroked my dick while I peeped the way her pussy peeked out under her ass cheeks. There was nothing sexier than how a woman was made.

She looked at me over her shoulder. Watching me as I ran my hand up and down my monster. She had tears all over her face and more dripping out of her eyes. "J.T., you gone put that in me? Huh, baby? You gone put all that dick in this yellow pussy and make me feel all better?" She popped her ass and pulled her cheeks apart. "You see that pink? You see hot wet you got me?" She smacked her own ass and I watched the cheeks jiggle.

By this time, my dick was standing up along my stomach. I was cocking him like a shotgun. Jennifer spun around, and grabbed him, kissing the head, before licking all around it. "This a lot of meat, J.T. This is a whole lot of dick right here. You gone have to force this in me to get it in. My hole might not let you. And what if it don't?"

She popped me back into her mouth and started to glide up and down my pole with so much spit in her mouth, it felt like I was already in her pussy. She rubbed my dick all over her lips and teeth, and I snapped. I pushed her back, and threw her thick ass leg and thigh on my shoulder. Put my dick on her entrance and pushed him in. As soon as I did, her back arched and she moaned so loud in my ear, it made me force him to her hot ass bottom. That pussy got to pulling at me right away.

Sucking like a vacuum cleaner. I pulled all the way out and slammed him back home and got to beating him in like a gangsta.

"Uhhhhhhh! J.T.! Wait! Wait, baby! You fucking me too hard! Wait! My pussy ain't ready for all that!

Uhhhhh!" She got to shaking so bad, I almost slipped out when I pulled my dick to her brim. "Shit! Fuck me, baby. I love you so much!"

Clap! Clap! Clap! My hips slammed into her center so fast, I could barely keep up with myself.

It felt good too. Nice and hot. I felt her muscles tugging at me and it made me want to come. I was trying my best not to but then, there it was, big globs too. So much, it made my stomach hurt. "Fuck, Jennifer! Damn, ma! This pussy so good, baby! Damn, this pussy fire!" I growled and threw her other leg on my shoulder, really beating it up with no mercy. She shook and screamed so much, she passed out under me, and I kept on going, fucking that pussy up. Ain't nothing like it.

* * *

Rip

I threw the bag on the floor and came out of my bedroom after closing the door behind me. I had to deal with this bullshit ass baby momma drama, and I didn't have no patience.

When I came out of the room, my baby mother, Vonna, was sitting at the dining room table with a frown on her face. She got up when I got halfway to her and put her hand on her hip. "I sho hope you got a good-ass excuse why you ain't make it to your daughter's doctor's appointment yesterday, after you promised me that you was coming. You see, I don't know why I be hanging on yo every word like you some kind of preacher or something. I be asking you to do the simplest of things, and you can't even do that. I simply said…"

I walked past her and even bumped her a little bit. I feel ain't feel like listening to all that chirping. Ladies, when a nigga been out in the streets all night long, I know it's annoyin' but before you tear into his ass, the first thing you should do is find out how much bacon he brought home. If the nigga ain't got shit, then you get on his ass. But, that nigga come into the house with a bag of money like I just did, then you praise him because that mean he care about you. He could have took that money to any other female's crib and she would have received him with open arms. The fact that he brought it to yours means he plans on getting you right first and foremost. Now my baby's mother was blowing me. I was ready to leave the crib and go somewhere where I knew I would be appreciated as a man.

"Oh hell, nall! I know you just didn't bump me like you want some drama like that. Nigga, we finna tear this whole house up." She got to taking off her earrings like she was really about to get down on me.

Smack! I dropped her ass straight to the floor. She landed on her ass and looked up at me, holding her face like she was hurt. I ain't feel shit because I was tired of her disrespectful ass mouth. I didn't tolerate that shit. I never came at her in that manner and I wasn't accepting her coming at me like that. "Shorty, I done told you one too many times about your tongue. Now, I hold you down like I'm supposed to. I pay every bill in this mafucka, and I'm gone always have you, because you got my daughter. But if you think I'm gone let you stand on my G, then you got another thing coming." I walked out of the dining room and left her ass on the floor, looking stupid.

Even though we had a daughter together, I really ain't love her like that. Me and Vonna was basically co-parenting, and fucking. I didn't see no future with her, and she probably didn't see none with me either. We were basically living in the moment and I was trying to make the best out it, until I decided what I was gone do about our situation. I just wanted the best for my daughter.

I opened her bedroom door and there she was, sitting on her bed, looking at her tablet. Five years old, and as beautiful as her freckle-faced mother. I guess Vonna had put beads all in her hair to match her clothes. They were red, black, gray, and clear. She still had on a Burberry 'fit I had bought her a few days ago, with the matching Jordans.

As soon as my daughter looked up and saw me, she dropped her tablet, and jumped from the bed right into my arms. "Daddeee, I missed you so much." She wrapped her arms and legs around my neck after I caught her. I held my baby for a long time just taking in a pure version of me. She was my everything.

"I missed you too, baby. But, I was thinking about you every single minute I was away. You're so special to me, and I love you with all of my heart." I kissed all over her until she started laughing and giggling. Vonna came into the room with an ice pack on her cheek. I thought, she was just being a drama queen, as usual. Any time I tried to spend some time with my daughter, she always found a way to barge in on us or break it up altogether. I think deep down, she was a little jealous of how I was with her. I know her and her father had a shady past. He was in and out of her life and a terrible liar.

"Baby can we do something as a family tomorrow, since we ain't seen you in a few days? I know that Bree would love that. Wouldn't you, baby?"

My daughter shook her head and hugged me tighter. "But Daddy, I just wanna do something with you, because Momma gone hog you. I never get to see you when I'm at school but she do and it's just not fair, because I love you too, even though I'm a kid."

"I'll tell you what. Tomorrow we can go anywhere you wanna go, Princess, and then later on that night while you're asleep, me and Mommy can go out, and we'll do what she wants to do. How does that some to everybody?"

Bree smiled and started kissing my cheek again and again, while Vonna looked like she was upset, mad and irritated. I didn't give a fuck. I loved my daughter, she's my everything. Me and Vonna would figure things out along the way. But, it was my job to make sure my daughter was mentally, emotionally, and financially stable at all times. It was the reason I was in those streets so hard and would continue to be.

After I put Bree to sleep, Vonna called herself wanting to sit me down so we could talk. I was tired as hell and really I didn't feel like hearing what she had to say. I needed to get some Z's if I was gone be able to hold up my promises to my daughter. I didn't care if I broke the ones I made about kicking it with her afterwards, I was solely concerned about Bree.

She came into the room and pulled the door up, sitting on the bed while I pulled the covers back, so I could climb under them. I had visions on getting a good night's sleep. I saw myself snoring and everything. "What's on your mind, Vonna?" I asked, taking my wife beater off.

Chapter 7

Rip

She stood up and rubbed my back. "I'm sorry about how I came at you back there. I gotta watch my mouth, the last thing I want to do is lose you. Our daughter loves you with all of her heart and so do I." She kissed my back, and then walked around to her side of the bed, turning on the lamp on her nightstand. I turned mine off.

"Shorty, I ain't tripping. I really don't like putting you in yo place like I did, but it just seem like you don't get shit. I ain't got time for that. You supposed to treat them fuck niggas out there like that. Not a man that's going out here every single day and putting his life on the line for the family, just to make sure we stay eating good. You know how much rent we pay in this mafucka?"

She shook her head, and then lowered it. "No, but I know it's a lot." She said this last part like she was afraid to admit it or something. "Baby, I don't want you to think that I don't appreciate you or something because I really do. It's just that sometimes being in this house fucks with my head. You know I used to run them streets just as much as you do, until I got pregnant with our daughter, and then you put a stop to all of that shit. But, don't think it's not still in me.

I hate being in this house all day long. It gets boring. After I get updated on social media, I be walking around here like an old woman."

I yawned. I mean, I heard what she was saying, but at the same time, I wasn't going for it. Wasn't no way she was finna be running them streets and my daughter ain't have her when she needed her, which in my opinion was all day long. Children had to be a priority, especially if you wasn't doing shit else, and she wasn't. I made sure she had more than everything she needed. "So, what you saying, Vonna, you wanna hit them streets again? And if so, to do what exactly?" I sat up in the bed, so I could see her more clearly.

She looked at me with her lil yellow face. Even in the dimly lit room, I could make out her freckles. I still thought she was fine though. But, she was one of those fines that you really couldn't appreciate after you got to know her, because the real her ruined it. She looked everywhere but at me.

"Go ahead and speak your mind. What you waiting on and make sure that you don't leave shit out."

"Well, I just think that you should let me at least…"

Boom! Boom! Boom! Boo-wa! Boo-wa! Boo-wa! Booooom! The windows of our bedroom shattered and more gunfire ensued. It felt like the house was being rocked. I fell to the floor and pushed Vonna on her stomach. Reaching under our bed, I grabbed a .40 Glock and slammed a fifty-round clip inside of it. Low crawlin' on my stomach, I made my way to my daughter's bedroom.

* * *

J.T.

I pulled into Fat Burger's parking lot and noted right away that it was full of niggas' cars I was used to seeing around my old hood. Just like I suspected, that nigga Looney was still scared of me. He had to have a million niggas just to do business. To me, that was coward shit. Whatever was gone happen was gone happen. I wasn't ducking no action. I wanted my woman back, and if that meant I was walking into a trap, I didn't give a fuck. So I parked, and all of the Blood niggas that ran under him, came and surrounded the whip I'd stolen only ten minutes prior. I let my seat back and didn't pay 'em no mind until Casey's fat ass started knocking on my window with his ashy ass knuckle.

The sun was out bright as hell. Before I jumped in the whip, I noted it was humid, and muggy. I hated weather like that, so I turned the A.C. all the way up, and tried to fight that off.

I rolled the window down enough to hear what this fat nigga had to say. "Whut up, Blood?"

"That nigga, Looney, said when you roll up, I gotta pat you down to make sure you don't be on no bullshit. All he want is the money. He ain't trying to make this a murder scene. So I gotta make sure you ain't packing."

I mugged that nigga like he'd lost his muthafucking mind. "Nigga, is you packing?"

He looked around, crazy. "Yeah, but I'm the enforcer, I gotta have a banger on me. How else I'm gone make sure Looney safe?" He looked like he was really waiting on me to give him that answer.

"Bro, you know damn well I'm packing. What the fuck I look like? Look, Casey, you niggas know how I get down. Now, if y'all on any bullshit, then we might as well get on dumb shit right now. All I want is my woman. Tell that nigga he can have that lil paper, no harm, no foul."

Casey shook his head. "Nall, Blood, we can't do the deal unless you give me your gun. I can't have my chief's life at risk fucking wit you. So, either give me the gun and let me pat you down, or ain't shit moving." All of the niggas surrounded my car with their hands under their shirts. I saw what it was right away. That nigga, Looney, had never thought about showing up.

He sent his lil henchmen to take my money, and then he was the type of nigga that would brag about it later on. I wasn't going for it. These niggas were gonna have to kill me in cold blood.

With the car still running, I made up my mind right then and there. I had to use my head in order to get out of the situation. I was glad I had made Jennifer stay at the hotel as much as she begged me to let her come. Had she been with me, I would not have been able to do what I was about to. I rolled the window all the way down and faced Casey.

"Look, bro, all I got is a hand pistol. This mafucka ain't even off safety, look."

As soon as he stuck his extra-pudgy-ass face into the car, I stuck the gun under his chin, and pulled the trigger. *Boo- wa!* His brains splattered all over the windshield. I threw the car in drive and pulled away after bussing out the passenger's window. I saw some nigga reach, but before he could, his brains was all over his chest and on the passenger's seat.

They started to let their toolies ride, shattering my back window and hitting the car with so many bullets, it sounded like hail was coming down from the sky like rain. I ducked low in my seat and stepped on the gas, heading straight into traffic, nearly slamming into a small yellow school bus carrying a bunch of kids wearing bright red helmets. My crazy ass took a few seconds to look them over, because I didn't really think the whole helmet thing was really real when it came to mentally challenged kids wearing them. I thought that was something people just said, but no, it was as real as Donald Trump becoming president.

Errrr-uh! I stepped on the gas again, and the Charger jumped the curb of the island in the middle of the busy street. I hit a U-turn, and then punched that bad boy. The Charger jerked and then took off like a rocket just as my phone rang, with Looney's face popping up on the screen.

* * *

Rip

More bullets chopped into my house, shattering damn near every window in the crib. I continued to low crawl on my way to my daughter's bedroom. Then I heard a loud boom and a bunch of footsteps. It sounded like the house was being invaded by an army.

"Ahhh! Dadddeee! Help me!"

"Bree!" I hollered and got up to run to her room. I didn't give a fuck if I got shot. I had to save my daughter, I was her only hope.

Boo-wa! Boo-wa! Boo-wa! The bullets slammed into the wall in front of me, and I fell to my knee and bussed my gun, finger fucking the trigger like a filthy whore.

Boom! Boom! Boom! Boom!

The masked man flew into the wall, hollered out and fell on his face. As I stepped over him, I bussed again and knocked in the back of his head, before leaning down and picking up his MAK-90. He had a clip in there so long, it looked like a silver two-by-four. I cocked it at the top and started spraying shit. It had to be about ten people in my house at once. I got to hitting anything that wasn't supposed to be there, while I made my way to daughter's room upstairs.

Boom-Boom-Boom! I knocked one nigga's chest off that was trying to creep up behind me. He fell to his knee and still tried to aim his gun. *Boom-Boom-Boom!* He flew backward and landed on his neck. I started to run up the stairs again.

"Dadddeeee! Help me! Please!"

"Shut up, you little bitch! You're coming with us!"
I heard the voice say from downstairs say.

What the fuck! I thought to myself, extremely
confused, being that I was headed up the stairs. I turned
around and jogged back down them as I heard the back
door of our crib being unlocked and plenty of footsteps.
My heart pounding like a fist in my chest. I could barely
breathe.

"Rippppp! Help me!" Vonna screamed out.

Shit! Save her or my lil' girl. Her or my lil' girl!
Fuck that! I had to save my daughter first. *She* needed
me, she was only five. She was most important. I flew
down the stairs and ran toward the back door.

As soon as I got to it and down the stairs, I saw her
being thrown into a big black Navigator. The doors
slammed, and then the truck was speeding away, sending
smoke into the air.

Booooommmm! Something exploded inside the
house with so much intensity, it sent me three feet into
the air. I landed on my back and shot right up. The house
was on fire, but I had to save my baby's mother. Fuck
that. I could not and would not let her die. I was already
on the verge of breaking down over my daughter. I
couldn't fathom how losing Vonna would make me feel.

"Riiipppp! Help me! Where are you?" she
screamed, as I ran through the flames back into the
kitchen.

"Shorty, where you at? What room are you in?"
The flames shot up, and nearly burned my face off. I
could feel the fire on the back of my neck, and it was
hard for me to breathe, because of what I was inhaling.
The smoke was dangerous, and thicker than a stripper
from Houston.

"In the front room. I can't move, they shot me in
both of my legs. Hurry up, baby! Please! I need you!"
Now I was running full speed, directly to the front of the

house. I saw her, lying on the floor, trying her best to crawl away from the couch that was on fire. The flames were tall as basketball players. The entire room had smoke pouring out of it. I could hear her choking and struggling to breathe.

Whooooosh! A big ass ball of fire shot up right in front of me and set my shirt on fire. I hurried and took it off, duckin' down and grabbing her by the leg, pulling her to me until I picked her up and ran full speed all the way out of the house.

I dropped her in the back yard and ran back into the house, up to our room. The flames hadn't made it that far, or at least I didn't think they had. I took the stairs two at a time, until the banister gave way and I almost fell.

Keeping my balance, I kept it moving until I got into the smoke-covered hallway. I ran and kicked the guest bedroom door in and snatched the bag of money, then went to the second-floor window and raised it. The smoke inside the house immediately rushed to get out. I could feel the heat on my back. My entire face was drenched in sweat. So much so, it looked like I'd played a full game of basketball in the summer sun.

As soon as I got the window all the way open, I tossed the bag of money out, slowly climbed out, and hung down with my back facing the yard. I wanted to get as low to the ground as possible before I decided to let go. It wasn't a long jump, but one I really didn't want to make.

Dooooom! "Ahhhhh, shit!" The blast sent me flying into the air.

Chapter 8

Lil Momma

"Ow! Ow! Looney, what the fuck is wrong wit you?" I asked as I tried to get away from him the second time. He'd grabbed a handful of my hair and yanked me from the bed while I was sleeping. Dragging me until I dropped to the floor with him, pulling me across it like a rag doll.

"Bitch!" He grabbed me by the throat and picked me up into the air, taking his gun and placing it to my forehead so hard, it stung. The hard steel felt like it was trying to go through the bone. I could smell his deodorant, and the aftershave he used.

I wiggled my legs, trying to get him to drop me. Yet, all he did was pick me all the way up and look at me like he hated my guts, and everything I stood for. "Let me go, Looney. What the fuck is your problem this morning?" I whimpered.

He cocked back his hammer. "That bitch-ass nigga think it's a game. He don't think I'll knock yo shit out and make his momma deliver yo brains to him? Mafucka think he can kill my cousin, and body a few of my niggas and ain't shit gone happen? Huh? Is that what he think?" he hollered into my face and threw me across the room.

I landed into the dresser. My back hit it so hard, it nearly knocked the wind out of me. Before I could gather myself, he came and grabbed me by the hair again, yanking my head backward. I felt the sharp pain shoot all along the back of my neck, and down my spine. Then, I was in the air again.

Whoom! Tisshhh! He threw me into the mirror hanging on the back of the door, shattering it. I could barely breathe. I turned on my side and tried to get up with glass all over me. I could feel it under the palms of my hands. It crunched, and some even cut into me, but I had to get out of that bedroom or I felt like he was going to kill me somehow.

He picked me up again and looked directly into my face with a menacing scowl. "Bitch, I don't get it. I know this nigga love you like a mafucka, so why he ain't drop that paper? Why did he go the route of shooting my niggas? What, he ain't fucking wit you like that no more or something?"

He had me by the throat and had a handful of my hair at the same time. I was scared. I didn't know what to say or do after he told me J.T. didn't pay the ransom. I couldn't do nothing but cry. The tears started to come out of my eyes right away.

"What are you talking about?"

Looney jerked me a little bit. "Bitch, I'm telling you that I ain't got that money, and I am supposed to have had it already but instead, all I got is two dead bodies, and another homie that's holdin' on for dear life. What the fuck is going on?"

He turned his head to the side and looked me over closely as I hung in the air.

"Looney, I don't know. Maybe he was worried about something. I know J.T. got me, though. Just let me talk to him. Let me tell him to come get me. If I can do that, then he'll handle that business right away. He probab..." I didn't even have time to brace for the blow. *Slap!*

He dropped me, and I fell to the floor on my back, with my eyes closed. I curled into a ball immediately.

"The next time I get in touch with that nigga, and he don't bring me my muthafuckin' money, I'm killing yo ass, bitch! I should do it now, 'cuz it seem like he ain't fucking witchu on that level no more." He slammed the

70

bedroom door after pushing Jamie into the room. She fell to her knees, almost on top of me.

I cried my eyes out. I started praying that J.T. still loved me. I prayed he hadn't turned his back on me, or had moved on without me. But, it just didn't seem right. If he had went to the meeting place and chose to body some niggas, instead of paying the money, then it must've meant shit didn't look right to him.

He was very intuitive when it came to parts of the game. Very seldom did he make a mistake. I just had to hold on to my faith that he would come for me when the time was right.

* * *

J.T.

"Let's go, Ma, we gotta get the fuck out of here right now. I done already switched whips." I took all of the blankets and sheets and balled them up, throwing them on the floor by the door, so they would be the first thing the housekeeper saw when she entered the room.

Jennifer had been on the bed watching television, but when she saw me, she jumped up with her eyes wide open. She looked past me, I guess to see if Lil Momma was with me. After reading my face, she started to get dressed, with a look on her face that said she was worried.

As soon as we got into the Explorer I'd stolen from about three blocks away, she placed her seat belt around her, and covered her face with her hands, sobbing into them.

I swallowed hard. "What's good, Jenn?"

She shook her head. "I already know something ain't right. Why isn't she with you? What did Looney do to her? Where is she? I want to see my cousin so bad, it hurts. I miss her so bad." She broke down. If I hadn't been entering the ramp onto the highway, I would have pulled over and did my best to console her. I hated hearing a woman cry. It was ten times worse for me, if I cared about the woman. And I cared about Jennifer a lot.

I reached over and rubbed her back. "Look, just relax. You know I'mma figure this shit out. I would have had her with me right now, but shit just looked super fishy to me. We ain't got no two hundred bands to risk throwing away to that nigga if he ain't gon' give her back to us." I grabbed her hand and kissed it. "I ain't see her nowhere in sight, so we finna have to do this shit *my* way. Every nigga in the world got people in they life that they care about that means more than any amount money. Looney got one of the two people that mean more than the world to and I'm finna go and snatch up one he'd go to war for. It's time he feel this shit.

I stepped on the gas, and Jennifer took my hand and interlocked her fingers inside of my own. She rubbed my hand against her wet cheek. "I trust you, J.T. Whatever you got up your sleeve, I just want you to know that I trust you, and I'm gon' to do whatever it takes to get my cousin back."

I looked her over closely. "You sure about that? Shit finna get real."

She looked at me for about five seconds, before slowly nodding her head. Her curly hair bounced, and her face turned into a smile.

* * *

Lil Momma

"Are you okay, girl?" Jamie asked, rubbing my back as I laid on my side. She had been asking me the same question for what seemed like an hour. I didn't know if she was genuinely concerned, or just worried about something. Either way, she was incredibly persistent.

Personally, I felt like shit. I was at another man's disposal and at any minute, he could end my life. I'm telling you, it's an indescribable feeling. You feel like trash, and no one can save you. You think about what the rest of the world is doing, and how happy they must be, when all along, you're trapped and on the verge of being murdered. Being helpless is the worst feeling in the whole wide world.

Jamie rubbed my back a little harder. "Hey, it can't be that bad." She was quiet for a little while and then I heard her moving around. "You know, when he get to fuckin' me up like he doin' you, there is only one thing that makes me feel better. This shit right here."

I looked over my shoulder at her. She held a brown package in her hand, shaking it a little bit to emphasize her point.

I narrowed my eyes at it, and then gave her a look that said, she must have been out of her rabid-ass mind. "Girl, what the fuck is that?" I asked, sitting up.

She smiled and licked her juicy lips. "This that shit that will take you away from here. He can whoop your ass all day long but if you're on this, you won't feel a thing. On top of that, it takes you to paradise. You'll feel like a fucking queen. It's the best." She closed her eyes and hugged herself.

I had to scoot backward, just so I could see her more clearly. She looked so happy. I found myself intrigued. "But what is it though?"

"This is what they call dog food." She shook it and adjusted her shoulders. "I'm gon' show you how it works."

She went into her waistband and pulled out what looked like a whole party kit. I saw a syringe, a burnt-ass spoon, a lighter, and something that looked like a mini rope. She took the powder and poured some of it onto the spoon, before dropping what I assumed was water onto it. Then she took her lighter, flicked it, and put the flame under the spoon, until all of the powder began to bubble as if she was frying it. Once the spoon turned red, she took a piece of cotton and placed it into the liquid on the spoon. She stuck the needle's point into that, and drew it up into the syringe. "Girl, help me wrap this thing around my arm." She asked, referring to the mini rope.

I didn't know why she wanted me to help her, but I did. I watched her stick the needle into a thick vein in her arm, before pushing the feeder down. As the liquid went into her, her eyes rolled into the back of her head. She moaned out loud and licked her lips.

As soon as I thought that she was in a faraway zone, I put my hand all the way in the air. *Smack!* I hit her ass hard. Then I brought it down again. She flew backward, after yelping out in pain, holding her face, looking at me like I had lost my mind.

"Bitch, you in here doing heroin! What the fuck is yo problem? Yo brother gon' kill yo ass when he finds out. And what about your daughter?" I ran over to her on my knees and smacked her again. *Smack!*

She scooted back on her ass and tried to get away from me. Her eyes were as big as Frisbees. She tried to get up and I tackled her back to the floor. We wrestled around, and I wound up on top of her. I slapped her again.

"Stop, Lil' Momma! Get the fuck off me. I was just trying to show you what I do to escape the pain," she whimpered, before I slapped her dumb ass again.

"Now, you listen to me, bitch. We finna get the fuck out of here. We gotta leave this nigga before he kill us, and you gotta get some help. Your daughter needs you, because y'all momma already too far gone. So, you gotta trust me and let me help *you and me*."

Jamie shook her head. "No, because even if we get away, he gone find us and kill us. I know him. That nigga is crazy.

It ain't nowhere we can run to," she whimpered. She sat back on her ass crying and then, she nodded out like she had fallen asleep.

I looked at this bitch like she was crazy. I mean, she literally nodded out, while we were in the middle of a conversation. Now, I don't know about you, but to me that was rude as fuck. So, you already know what I did, licking the palm of my hand first to make sure I got the message across. *Smaaaccck!*

My wet hand connecting with her face was so loud. It sounded like I'd struck her on the back. She fell onto her back, covering her face with her hands crying like a big baby. "You gotta find a new move, Lil Momma. That shit hurt!"

"I'm sorry, boo, but I gotta know if you wit me. I gotta know if you gon' ride wit me against this nigga and if so, we gotta come up wit a plan to make sure that we get away. 'Cuz if we make one mistake, one thing is for sure, he'll definitely kill us."

* * *

Rip

I fell to my knees and the tears wouldn't stop coming. My chest heaved up and down and I felt like I was getting ready to throw up. I didn't remember the last time I'd cried and yet here I was, breaking down in the hospital's bathroom. Missing my daughter, worrying about her, and trying to put the pieces of the puzzle together.

Ghost

I had fucked over so many heavy hitters in the
name of that paper, I didn't know who was clapping at
me. My mind was fucked up. My brain was more
clouded than a car full of weed smoke. I bounced back
and forth on my knees as I imagined my baby girl's face.
Her little fingers and toes, her kisses and the way she felt
in my arms. There was nothing more perfect in life than
her.

I tried to get up but wound up falling back down.
My knees were weak, and my vision was clouded. It was
my job to protect her. It was my job to make sure she
was always safe and sound, and I had failed her
miserably. What kind of father allowed his child to be
taken without dying, trying to keep her safe? Fuck! I felt
like a pussy. I missed my baby.

Vonna turned out to be okay. She took a shot to the
thigh and had only suffered few burns across her back. I
figured her scars would make me love her more. I started
to appreciate her for bringing our daughter into the
world. I wished I had seen things more clearly before our
attacks, but sometimes it took shit like this to happen
before a man got the full picture.

It wasn't until four hours later, before I was able to
creep up the stairs to her floor and see her. I couldn't
stroll in there as a visitor, because I knew that this crime
would be investigated. So, I waited until the middle of
the night, snuck up there and closed the door behind me.
She was sleeping like a baby. She had IV's all in her
arms, and a machine that kept on beeping every second
or so.

I hated seeing her like that. She looked like a
grown version of my daughter, which made a few tears
sail down my face. I walked over to her and kissed her
on the forehead.

She opened her eyes slowly, blinked them a few
times, and then smiled. "I knew you would come to me,

76

Rip." Her voice sounded hoarse. She coughed and turned further onto her side.

The medical staff already had her slightly on her right side. I guessed so the burns on her back would not be affected by the bed, but I didn't know for sure. I kissed her on the lips. Even though they were dry, they were the most beautiful in the whole world to me. "Baby, I'm sorry about all of this. I wish you didn't have to go through this." More tears sailed down my cheeks. I hated seeing her in that bed like that. I knew it was all my fault. I had failed my family. I felt like shit.

Vonna coughed and tried to catch her breath. I reached on to the side table and grabbed the juice, placing the straw to her lips, so she could sip out of it. Once she had her fill, she smacked her lips together and groaned. I could tell that she was in obvious pain.

I leaned down and laid my head on her chest, before kissing her soft cheeks. "Baby, I love you, and you already know I ain't finna take this shit lying down. I'm finna get our daughter back, and I'm gone make these muthafucka pay for offending our family. You know how I get down." I wiped the tears away from my cheeks, and then hers.

"I know you are, Rip. I know you a beast, baby. I'm just scared, that's all." She coughed and then licked her thick lips. I could still see where the red lipstick had once been. Now, it looked faded. "I don't want to lose you, Rip. I really, really love you and I always will. But, I know I gotta release you into that world, so you can go get our daughter back. I trust you, baby." She started coughing and crying at the same time.

I put the juice back to her lips and allowed her to drink. I rubbed her forehead and kissed her cheeks again and again. I fell in love with my baby's mother all over again as I looked down on her in that bed. I knew I would do anything for her from that point on. I had to hold her down. I had to protect her and make sure that nothing or no one ever harmed her again.

That was my job and I would not take it lightly. I felt my heart beating so hard in my chest, I had to kneel down. That only happened when I knew I was getting ready to go on a murder spree. There was only one organization that I knew who had enough firepower to come at me the way they did, and I was about to go at them with everything I had until I got my daughter back.

Chapter 9

J.T.

"It's just crazy, because I never seen you on campus before. But, Melanie did say something about one of her peoples coming down here this month. She had to be talking about you, because she said it was gone be a dude. I thought she said her brother, but I could be wrong," the nerdy white dude said, before adjusting his glasses on his nose. He looked like Sheldon from *The Big Bang Theory*.

I kept my neck stiff as a board and adjusted my own glasses on my nose. I was having a tough time seeing out of them. I caught them off the last dude I'd jacked. He must have worn bifocals because them mafuckas was hurting my head.

The white dude turned the lock and pushed in the door to the dorm room. "Now, I usually don't do this, but I know she's been wanting to see you. We're in the same Biology Club, and it's all she could talk about for weeks. I think she'll be very happy to see you."

"Do you know when she's scheduled to be back?" I asked, stepping into her room. She had all kinds of Chris Brown posters. She also had pictures of Ariana Grande, and posters from the movie, *Raised as a Goon*.

He adjusted the glasses on his nose again. "Well, her last class ends in about twenty minutes. She usually stops to get a bite to eat, and then comes straight back to her room to take a nap."

I gave this dude a look that told him he had been watching her way too closely. He must have picked up on it because he lowered his head and shook it. "I know, I have way too much time on my hands. But, I can't help it. She is way too pretty. She's all can think about." He looked up at me as if he were scared. "Geez, I sure hope I didn't offend you."

Had she been my little sister, my woman or somebody like that, I would have already knocked him clean out. I could only imagine what he did in her room when she was in class and he was roaming around with plenty time on his hands.

I looked around and tried to determine if she had a roommate or not. I couldn't really tell. There were two beds, but only one of them was made up. That didn't necessarily mean she didn't have a roommate. It could have meant her roommate was doing laundry somewhere. "Does she have a roommate?"

Sheldon smiled. "Yeah, and she's just as hot." He jumped back. "Whoa, I'm sorry, man. I didn't mean that."

I could hear the rain pouring down outside. They had left their window open in the room, so I could hear the rain attacking the pavement outside. I could also smell it.

I couldn't let this dude leave out of my sight. All it would have taken was for him to see Melanie and tell her that I was waiting for her in her room. She'd think it was Looney and call him, find out it isn't and freak out, and I'd be busted before I could even use her for leverage. Fuck that, I wasn't slipping up like that.

"Say, where is the bathroom?"

He stepped all the way into the room and closed the door behind him. "That door right there. It's all pink inside, and they are so clean. The shower curtain is see-through, and I can't believe how they get dressed in the morning, with both of them being in there at one time. It's so cool."

Now y'all might think I'm bullshitting, but that is what this dude actually said. I shook my head and snatched him into a bear hug, before head-butting him in the face and dropping him.

His glasses flew under the bed and he landed on his back, with blood coming out of his nose. Both hands covered his face and he made noises like he was in agony. "Uhhh! Uhhh! You broke my nose, man. I didn't mean what I said, honest." He tried to scoot backward on his butt to get away from me, but he bumped into the bed.

"Look man, I don't wanna hurt you, but I gotta put you to sleep for a lil minute while I holler at my people. If you be cool right now and don't say another word, I won't kill you. But, if you say anything, I gotta body you." I started to walk toward him.

He jumped to his feet and tried to run toward the door. "I said I was sorry, man. You're a freaking lunatic." I dove and grabbed his shirt, ripping it, but still managing to pull him back to me. As soon as his back hit my chest, I wrapped him into a sleeper hold and put so much pressure into it, I could hear him choking. I lowered my arm and wrapped it around his Adam's apple, pulling it backward toward me.

"I told you not to say nothing. You just had to open your mouth. Now, I gotta do what I gotta do."

I wasn't into killing mafuckas senselessly, so I had to imagine he was Looney. I went from thinking that to imagining him peeping in on them girls and pleasuring himself to them.

That shit got me heated. I knew dude had to be some kind of pervert. He knew way too much about their apartment. So, I choked him with all of my might, as he tried to jerk and fight me off of him, but it didn't do no good. I thought about Looney touching Lil Momma. I thought about his bitch ass touching Jennifer, or anybody trying to hurt either one of them, and squeezed harder and harder. I would never let nobody hurt them again once I got Lil Momma back. I would rather die first.

I squeezed and squeezed, until I knew he had to be dead. I got up about ten minutes later, after my arm went numb. I pulled him off of the bed and dropped him to the floor. Then, I rolled him under it, got up and stood behind the door, waiting for Melanie to get back.

* * *

Rip

Whoom! "Bitch-ass niggas! Everybody get the fuck down, and I ain't playing either!" I said, after kicking in the big brown door of the traphouse.

I had two .40 calibers in my hands and I wasn't playing no games. These was my Crip niggaz, and I didn't give no fucks. They had all been caught off guard, because after the door was kicked in, they started to run for cover.

I knew this spot only had one exit, the door I had come through and was standing in front of heavily armed. "Where the fuck is that nigga, Loc?" I asked, waving the guns around at about ten niggas that was on their backs, looking up at me like I was crazy.

Some dark nigga with a blue rag over his face was mugging me so hard, I felt like he was trying to test my gangsta. He pulled his rag down so that it was around his neck. "Say Cuz, ain't you one of us?"

Boom! Boom! Boom! The bullets ripped into his chest and knocked him on his side. He started shaking like a fish out of water. The other niggas looked like they wanted to break out of the house.

"Now, I'm gone ask you lil bitch niggas one more time. Where the fuck is that nigga, Loc, at?" I pointed the gun at some yellow skinny nigga that probably thought he was Snoop or something. Before he even started talking, I already knew I was finna pump his ass full of lead. I didn't like his tough guy posturing. "You got something you wanna say nigga?"

He curled his upper lip. "Anybody can talk all that shit when they got the ups on a mafucka. But, put them pistols down and I promise you, I'll show you that you ain't on shit. That's on my rag, Cuz.

I turned my head to the side to really get a good look at this lil' nigga. He had plenty heart. I wished I had known him before that day. I would have loved to put him down on a few missions, but life didn't work out like that. I put the pistol straight to his forehead and pulled the trigger twice.

Boom! Boom!

His noodles busted out the back of his head and stained the carpet. He had plenty shit in there too. It made a big ass mess. I was mad at him for fucking the floor up. "Yo, you ain't have to do that shit, Cuz. That was my brother. He kinda thrown off up top, now he gone. My mother gone..."

Boom! Boom! Boom! All three bullets ate away his face. He flew backward and that was the last I heard from him. I didn't like all that whining and shit. That irritated me.

"I'm gone ask this room one more time, do any of you niggas know where Loc at?" I already bodied three, it was seven more to go, and the way I was missing my daughter, it wouldn't have been no problem.

A lil' boy that couldn't have been no older than fifteen spoke up. "Man, he over on Ventura Place. He dropped us off this work and we supposed to work for two days straight, until he get back here. I don't know what yo beef is with him, Cuz, but I just got jumped in. I don't wanna die." He swallowed and looked me in the eye.

I looked around at the rest of the lil bangers. "Is he telling the truth? Is that nigga over on Ventura? Huh? Somebody better co-sign this shit or it's about to get a lil' bloodier. Tell me somethin'."

It seemed like everybody was trying to talk at once, confirming what the lil homie had told me. I couldn't do nothing but shake my head. The only thing worse to me than a whiny-ass nigga, was a snitch nigga, a mafucka that couldn't hold his own weight and chose to relay information, instead of stand on his gangsta. I felt sick on the stomach. The shit pissed me off.

Boom! Boom! Boom! Click-Click. Chicka! Cock-Cock. Boom! Boom! Boom! There was so much smoke, I could barely see. The pistols felt hot in my hand.

Boom! Boom! Boom! Click-Click.

I looked around the room with my chest heaving up and down. A whole room full of snitches dead. I felt like I had done the world a favor.

* * *

J.T.

I saw the bedroom door opening. "Melanie, baby? Are you here yet?" came a male's voice. I dipped back into the bathroom but held the door open enough so I could see into the room.

Some big ass nigga that looked like a football player eased into the room and hung up his jacket. He had on a USC football jersey. I wondered if he played there or not. I didn't know, but I was ready to take a good look at him. As of today, his career was about to be over. I started to imagine him being Looney right away.

He took his jersey off and walked around the room in a tight-ass wife beater. The mixed stud had muscles on top of muscles. Now, I was ripped up, but this dude looked like he took that shit to a whole 'nother level.

After he slipped off his pants, he walked around the room in only his boxers, singing Bruno Mars, "That's What I Like." I couldn't do nothing but laugh a little bit at that. He put on some music and looked like he was on his way to the bathroom.

I hopped into the tub and closed the shower curtain back, and that's when I remembered that "Sheldon" had said the curtain was see-through.

Fuck, I thought. I just prayed this goofy nigga didn't look in my direction. He came into the bathroom shortly after, lifted the toilet seat, and started to piss. I looked up and tried to gather my thoughts. I had to figure out a way to strategically attack him. But then, something caught my eye.

Right in the corner of the ceiling over the shower was a little red light. I looked closer and sure enough, it was what I thought it was. A fucking camera. The first person I thought about was dead-ass "Sheldon." That sick son of a bitch.

Dude's big beefy ass finished pissing and washed his hands, before drying them and looking at his teeth in the mirror. I was just about to jump out and attack him, when the front door opened, and he left out of the bathroom.

"Fuck, Kammy, you beat her here?" he asked.

She sounded out of breath. "Yeah, I made her take my car to get an oil change, and the tires rotated. We got about a half an hour. Let's make it work."

The next thing I heard was a bunch of kissing and moaning. Then clothes being ripped off and more kissing, more moaning.

"Ooh, shit. I been waiting for this all day long. I been wanting you to fuck me so bad. I want that huge cock deep in my pussy. I love it," she moaned.

"Yeah, I know you do. Bend over the bed and hold yourself open for me. I wanna fuck your ass like I did Saturday. It felt so good." I heard a loud smack and then she yelped loudly.

"Ahhhh, shit, just hurry. The lube's in my nightstand. I need you up in there."

I heard a bunch of rattling around, and then she moaned so loud, my dick got hard. I slowly closed the bathroom door and left it open just enough so I could peek in at them.

I saw the big light-skinned nigga had the white girl by her waist, fucking her with anger. I mean, he was pounding into her so hard it sounded like thunder. He was tearing that ass up and she was screaming for him to do it harder.

"Fuck me, Jake! Yes! Fuck my white ass harder! Oh, I love it so much! I love your black cock up my ass! Fuck this white bitch. Pleeease, uh!" She had tears in her eyes, slamming back into him while his dick went in and out of her asshole.

The big nigga's chest muscles were jumping, his arms clenching off and on. He looked like he was on a mission to fuck that ass over, and he was succeeding.

"I'm cumming, Jake! Oh. My. Fucking. Gawd. I'm cumming! So hard!" She smashed back into him.

He grabbed a handful of her hair, making her arch her back, and fucked her like a monster. "I'm cummin' too! Oh shit, I'm cummin' in your ass, Kammy. I'm cummin' all in this pink booty, and it's awesome!" He slammed into her harder and harder.

The bed was rocking back and forth. Books fell off of the shelves in the room, and then he fell on top of her.

"My pussy. My pussy, Jake. Please put your black dick in my cunt and fuck it until it's raw. Please. I'll give you anything that I have. Just hurry before she gets back. I need you."

Jake pulled out of her ass and flipped her onto her back. She put her knees to her chest, and I could see her pink pussy pop all the way out, leaking. I had never seen a white girl's pussy in real life before and hers looked good. It looked like it was brand-new or something. My dick was super hard. It didn't look better than a black one to me, but just on some real shit, that mafucka looked good.

Jake took his dick, which looked like it was about nine inches, and started to stuff it into her. The further he got in, the louder she screamed, until he was all the way in and she started to cry. "Choke me now, Jake. While you're fucking me. Just choke me and take my pussy."

Jake took his hands and wrapped them around her neck and squeezed until her face turned red. Then he got to stroking that pussy hard. I could hear the sounds of her juices, it sounded like somebody was in the room chewing gum loud as hell. I never even knew white girls' pussies got that wet.

"Oh shit! I'm cumming, Jake! Choke me harder. I'm cumming! I'm cumming so fucking hard right, ack-ack-ack!"

Jake got to killing that pussy and then he hollered out and fell on top of her. I waited until they started to kiss, before I stepped out of the bathroom.

I was just about to smack him upside the head with the pistol, when the front door opened in a flash and Melanie ran in and jumped right on top of Kammy.

"You fucking bitch, I knew you were going behind my back and screwing my man. I should have never trusted you."

I stepped back into the bathroom and watched them as they rolled around on the bed. Jake got up and closed the door. As they were rolling around, Kammy was giving up crazy shots of her lil pink pussy. Her ass and kitty was wide open. That shit looked crazy.

"Get off me, Melanie. I can explain everything if you just give me a chance to," Kammy cried out.

They fought for hand control and then Melanie got on top of her and slapped her face. "I can't believe you. After I left Adam completely alone, because you said you liked him. You send me away so you can fuck my man?" She slapped her again, this time so hard it brought blood to her lip.

Jake ran over and picked her up off of her and Kammy got up and ran in the kitchen and grabbed a knife.

"You get off of me, Jake, you cheating bastard. How could you, after I gave you my virginity? I thought you loved me."

"I do love you, Melanie, it's just that you barely ever want to put out and Kammy's a whore. She loves to fuck just as much as I do. It doesn't mean anything, honest."

"You son of a bitch!" Kammy ran at him full speed and slammed the knife into his back, making him drop Melanie.

"Awwww! What the fuck is your problem!" He backhanded her, and she flew across the room with the knife still in her hands. "This crazy bitch just stabbed me!"

Kammy jumped up and ran over, plunging the knife in his back again.

Chapter 10

J.T.

Kammy pulled the knife out and slammed it right back into him. His head jerked backward, then he fell face-first on the bed while blood leaked out of his back like Kool-Aid. "You son of a bitch, you took my virginity too, and you told me that you loved me. How dare you talk about me like I'm some average slut that you and all the Trojans have run through? I deserve some respect!" She attempted to stab him again, but Melanie jumped in, and they held the knife way up in the air, struggling for it.

"Let it go, you crazy bitch. You probably fucking killed him. Oh my God. You probably killed Jake. The whole school is going to be pissed at you."

Tears started to run down Kammy's cheeks. She frowned, and I could tell she was in some form of emotional pain. I think she really liked the mixed dude or whatever, because she kept looking down on him and every time she did, more tears came.

I was thinking about going out there and breaking it up, but I decided to let things play out. I wanted to see where they was about to go.

"Kammy, just give me the knife. We can still make some sense of all this. You don't have to go out this way." Melanie grunted and struggled against her.

I don't know if finally, Kammy just gave in, or didn't care anymore, but she released the knife and covered her face with her hands, while she cried beside him on the bed. Jake laid flat on his stomach with his eyes closed. I was low-key hoping he was dead. That way, I didn't have to kill him.

As soon as Melanie took the knife away with her right hand, she pushed the shit out of Kammy with her left hand so hard, she landed on the floor on her side. Melanie jumped out of the bed and looked down on her. "You fucking bitch, I trusted you. I told you the way I felt about him, and you still went behind my back and betrayed me. I should kill you, just like you probably did him."

Kammy looked up to her with hatred in her eyes. She came to a kneeling position, with her tanned titties jiggling on her chest. I could still make out the bra strap line where the sun was not able to tan. There was one of them on each shoulder.

"You think I'm scared of you, Melanie? You stupid bitch, I was fucking him the second day after you introduced us. I knew that I liked him right away. He's the fucking quarterback. He has a future, and it's not supposed to be with some ghetto hoodrat out of L.A. What do you want, for him to try and visit you and get caught in a drive-by?

There's a reason why when guys like him leave the hood, they wind up with white girls like me. It's because I'm a long-term vacation, and you black whores aren't anything but pull-me-downs. So, yeah, I was fucking him. I had him all up my cunt and my ass, and it was awesome."

Melanie began to sob, snot running out of her nose. She looked hurt. "But, I thought you were my friend, Kammy. I thought we were cool."

Kammy stood all the way up and laughed. "Puh-lease. You can't offer me anything. Everybody knows that when you get to college, it's all about the connections you make. The only thing I can look forward to getting when I'm with you is weird looks from everybody, because I'm walking around with some ghetto hopeful. I feel sorry for you more than anything, because you're a nobody. Your pussy could never be as good as mine. Ever! You're a black bitch. You're nothing but..."

Whum! Whum! Whum! "Ahhh! I hate you! I hate you! I hate your fucking guts," Melanie screamed as she plunged the knife into Kammy's stomach three quick times. She closed her eyes and held the bloody knife tightly as her blood dripped from it.

Kammy fell slowly to her knees with her eyes wide open. She held her stomach and then looked down at her bloody hands. "I can't believe you did this," she struggled to say before falling forward on her stomach. A pool of blood formed around her, with her mouth left wide open.

I smiled. I couldn't believe that shit had worked out the way it did. I didn't have to do much. I looked over to Jake, and he looked like he was trying to get up. There was so much blood coming from him, the whole bed was drenched in it.

He got onto his knees. "Melanie, help me," he groaned, before falling back to his chest. He reached an arm out toward her and she took a step back, mugging him with hatred.

I couldn't believe my eyes. I guess the saying was true about a woman being scorned. That's why I always tried my best to not fuck over no female, because when they clapped back, they clapped back for real. That shit wasn't a game.

Melanie stayed there and watched him bleed out as if that had been her plan all along. Once he collapsed, and the light left out of his eyes, only then did she drop the knife and run over to the bed and hug him.

"I'm so sorry, Jake, please come back. Let's just go and get you some help. I need you, baby."

Ghost

All that was for nothing, because I could tell he was gone. I'd had enough of all of that. I came out of the bathroom with my gun pointed directly at her.

* * *

Rip

"Hey, Rip, how are you doing, baby? I ain't seen you in a while? How is your daughter?" Peaches asked and took a step to the side to allow me to come into her crib.

I stepped inside and looked around, noting that their two sons were home, and seated in the living room playing a video game.

I curled my lip at that because it made me think about my daughter. She didn't play video games like that, but she loved to sit in front of the TV and watch movies. "I'm doin' alright. Is that nigga, Loc, here?" I asked, while giving her a hug.

Peaches was super thick. I mean, she was the kind that was one sandwich away from being a big girl, but even if she had ate that sandwich, she would have still been fine as a muthafucka.

I thought most bigger girls were fine anyway. They just seemed like they had more swag about themselves. But Peaches, on most ordinary days had me lusting over her, like a pervert in a strip club for the first time. Even though I was there on business, I had to wrap her in my arms, just so I could feel her body against mine. She looked just like Angell Conwell from the show, *Family Time*.

"Yeah, he upstairs in the shower. He just went up, he should be down in about twenty minutes. Can I get you something to drink until then?"

She started walking toward the kitchen, and I couldn't help but to look down at that fat ass booty.

92

Damn, that mafucka was right. She had the type of ass that made a nigga just wanna know what it feels like to be hitting it from the back. Or to pick her up in the air and hold her by it. I wanted to sniff that mafucka, it was so big. "Yeah, I'll take some juice if y'all got some."

As soon as she left and went all the way into the kitchen, I took my .44 Desert Eagle out of the small of my back and turned it around, so I was holding the barrel, with the handle out front.

I looked down at their oldest son, who had to be about eleven. I raised my hand in the air and brought it back down with all of my might, slamming the handle into his jaw, knocking him out cold.

Before the other one could start crying, I scooped him up and put him in the sleeper hold while I kept my hand around his mouth. He was about nine. His legs kicked in the air until they stopped. Once I felt like he was out for the count I laid him on the floor next to his brother. I took the controller and fixed the game so that the computer was playing all by itself.

As Peaches was making her way into the living room, I met her halfway. I didn't want her walking in there and seeing her kids laid out like that. I figured that would have been rough for any mother to see. So, I met her with a hug and a kiss on the neck.

She shivered and looked up the stairs with a big smile on her face, before handing me the orange juice. "Boy, you better stop before you get me in trouble." Her pretty caramel face did its best not to blush. I thought that was cute as hell, even under the current circumstances.

I grabbed her into me, and she automatically wrapped her arms around my neck, breathing in my face ruggedly. Sitting the juice on the table, I reached around and gripped that big ass booty, squeezing it. It felt soft and had my piece hard as hell. When I gripped it, she moaned into my ear and I almost forgot why I was there. "You already know I'd tear this pussy up, don't you?"

She bit into her bottom lip and looked up at me in a zone, nodding her head slowly. She smelled like jasmine and hair care products. That's that hood shit I had grown up to love and appreciate.

"I just want to let you know I ain't gone hurt you more than I have to, but I came here on some business regarding my daughter, and your baby daddy wrapped up in this shit. Now, I done already put yo kids down."

Her eyes got bucked as hell, and she looked like she wanted to run into the living room to check on them, but I blocked her path. "Rip, please."

"Peaches, listen to me, man. They good, all I did was put them to sleep for a minute until I can do what I gotta do. Now, on the strength of you, I ain't gone kill them, or you. I know you a good ass mother, and you make sure they stay straight, and you ain't got nothing to do with these streets, but Loc do. So, I'mma give y'all a pass, but I'm finna fuck him over in front of you, just to show you what it's gone look like if you cross me by snitching on what happens to this nigga, okay?"

"That ain't even in me. I understand the game, just leave me and my kids out of this. Please, he don't do shit for us anyway. And quiet as it's kept, when you done, you still can get this pussy."

I laughed. I already knew that Peaches was stomp down. Her father had been a crazy kingpin nigga in the nineties, before he was murdered in front of her. Two years later, her mother was killed on her twelfth birthday. So, Peaches had been through a lot. I never heard about her in the hood running her mouth about nothing and she knew plenty shit, trust me.

I tied her and her kids to chairs, even though they were still knocked out cold, and I went upstairs and met that nigga, Loc, in the shower. When I opened the door, his fat ass was just turning off the water.

"Peaches, I'm glad you came up here. Bitch, I want you to suck this dick before I leave, and I don't know about giving you the rent this month. Don't you think it's about time you went out and got a job? I'm tired of taking care of yo lazy ass. And, I don't wanna hear you say that taking care of those kids is a job, because that's not what the fuck I mean. I mean a real ass job that pay the bills."

I stood there and crossed my arms with the pistol in my hand, just listening to this nigga. It was amazing how kats treated the women that had their children. They acted like since the child was born, it meant they didn't have to show the women respect, because she was bound to them for life no matter what.

My father was the same way, and it was the reason I could never respect him as a man. I got irritated quick. I pulled back the shower curtain and smacked the shit out of him with the pistol four times. *Whack! Whack! Whack!*

I grabbed him by the throat and pulled his naked ass out of the tub.

"You can have the money man. My safe open right now, it's fifty bands in there right now, just don't kill me, Cuz," he whined like a little bitch. Once again, I hated when a nigga did that. That shit got on my nerves, but I tried to keep my cool. I wound up dragging the nigga down the stairs by his throat, until he was in the basement, along with the rest of his family.

* * *

J.T.

"Look shorty, I don't wanna kill you. But at the same time, if you try and come at me bogus, I'm gone be forced to knock that head off.

Now, I need you to roll out wit me, because I got some business going on with your brother, Looney. I need you as a pawn. I don't wanna hurt you, but if I gotta put a bullet in you to let you know I'm serious, I most definitely will, because this shit bigger than you."

Melanie held her hands in the air with tears in her eyes. "J.T., what the fuck is going on? I thought you and my brother was cool. I thought you would always protect me, like you did when I was in high school. Why am I the enemy now, and no longer your little Barbie?"

I shook my head. "You are still my little Barbie, it's just business. Shit, I gotta handle with him, so let's go."

She blinked as more tears fell from her eyes. "What about them? Aren't you gonna turn me in?" She pointed to Kammy and Jake's dead bodies with her head.

I frowned. "Fuck them. That shit ain't got nothin' to do with me. I gotta get Lil' Momma back, and the only way I'm gone be able to do that is if I got you to trade in. I know that's fucked up to hear, but the truth is the truth. "

"Okay, but can I at least kiss Jake's lips one more time? It's the only way I'm going to be able to release him from my heart."

I saw the way she looked at me with pleading eyes, and I melted. Who was I to take that away from her? After all, that nigga had taken her virginity. I could only imagine what that meant to a female. So, I couldn't see myself stopping her from getting her last kiss, and I didn't.

Afterward, we strolled out of the room, with my arm around her neck and her head laid on my chest, until we got to the truck, and I told her the rules that would keep her alive.

Chapter 11

Lil Momma

Jamie kissed my neck, and I could feel her tongue snake its way into my earlobe. I spread my legs and she slid two fingers into me, running them in and out while I moaned into her face.

Her thumb was driving me crazy and for some reason, the feel of her soft skin against mine, only heightened my arousal.

Looney continued to stroke his huge penis while he stood over us, watching the whole scene we were forced to put on for him. Even though I hated going through the whole routine, I had to admit Jamie made it damn near bearable.

She did some things to my body that made me start to have second thoughts about ruling girls out.

"Yeah, I love watching you hoes get down. You bitchez gone fall in love with each other when I'm done." Looney continued rubbing his penis.

Bam! Bam! Bam!

There was a loud beating on the door, loud enough to make him jump into the air. He grabbed his gun off of the dresser and went to open it with an attitude. Jamie pulled her fingers out of my pussy and stuck them into her mouth. That made me question how much acting she was really doing as well.

"What? Melanie! Her campus? Well, where she at? Aw shit, man. Yo, that's my baby sister, man, we gotta hit these streets and find her. She all I got left in this world, besides my mother." He stepped out of the room and closed the door behind him.

As soon as he left out, Jamie lowered her face between my legs and started attacking my kitty like a true lesbian. I mean, she had me screaming and writhing all over the bed, with tears coming out of my eyes. I was shaking and had no control over how many times I came. Finally, I had to push her ass away from me. "Girl, move, that's enough. That nigga ain't even in here no more."

She sat back on her knees licking her lips and sucking her fingers loudly. "That's my bad. I just go into my zone, and when I do, I be in another world. I just enjoy being a pleaser, I been that way my whole life."

I stood up on shaky knees, trying to gather myself. I had juices running down my thighs and my kitty felt all tingly. Because they had shaved all of the hair off of her, my pussy kept sticking to my inner thighs. Every time I walked, it would force one lip to pull apart, and vice versa.

"Okay, something has happened, I just don't know what. Who is Melanie?"

Jamie stood up and stretched, her titties jiggled on her chest. She took her hand and slid it between her legs and smushed her pussy lips together. A small trace of clear gel oozed out. She scooped it onto her finger and licked it off. "I'm so fucking horny."

I rolled my eyes. "Jamie, snap out of that shit." I smacked her fingers away from her mouth and pulled her by the arm until she was sitting down on the bed, with me pacing in front of her. "Now tell me who the fuck is Melanie?"

She exhaled loudly. "That's his precious lil sister he is always talking about." She moved her head from side to side like a little girl at recess. "Melanie this, and Melanie that. Melanie goes to USC. Melanie is going to be a doctor. Melanie is the best woman in the whole wide world and Michelle Obama should look up to her." She opened her mouth and stuck her finger down in it to indicate it all made her sick.

I rolled my eyes again. "Well, clearly you don't like this bitch, but why would anybody want to do anything to her?"

As soon as I asked the question, I got it. I couldn't help smiling.

Jamie shrugged her shoulders. "Probably somebody that's tired of hearing Looney go on and on about her. I wish I could have been took her ass out the game. Oh, and I forgot, Melanie is a virgin. He always gotta mention that."

She was making me irritated. "Girl, shut up and turn that TV on over there."

She hopped up and stuck her fingers back in her mouth. I don't know what her issue was with my taste, but she obviously liked it a lot.

As soon as she turned the television on, we flipped to ABC, and there was breaking news on the USC campus. Apparently, they had found three students murdered. They were saying the school was on red alert and they were looking for multiple suspects. They weren't releasing any intimate details at the moment, but let the public know the investigation was on going, and they would release more information as it became available.

I flipped from channel to channel and they were all saying the same thing. I knew for a fact it was all J.T. I had no doubt in my mind that he was going on savage mode over me, and it made me feel like a princess. Men like him were hard to come by. He was the only man I knew for a fact I would kill anybody over, with no hesitation.

"Look, we gotta get out of here. I need to know where we are, so I can figure out what needs to be done. I think when Looney gets back here, he's going to act like a lunatic over her. Now, I don't know about you, but

I don't feel like gettin' my ass whooped over her. And you know he's going to beat both of us."

She plopped on the bed and put her leg up, unintentionally showing off her kitty, I figured. "Yeah, you're right because every time he gets mad, he always finds a way to fuck me up. I'm tired of all that. I just want to be happy." She blinked, and tears sailed down her cheeks.

"Okay, so we gotta put a plan in motion. Who is here right now?" I asked, pacing.

"I think Tommy is out there now. He's supposed to be some kind of house bodyguard over us. But, I got him wrapped around my finger. He'll do anything I say, long as he can sneak and get some pussy in return. His dick is small though, I mostly get sick with him on top of me, so I don't wanna go that route if I don't have to."

I raised my right brow. "Would you rather stay around and see how long it'll be before Looney kills one or the both of us?" I gave her a look that said she had better get her shit in order.

She lowered her head. "Okay, so what do you want me to do?"

I must have paced for another five minutes before it all came to me. "Listen, this is what you're gonna do, and I'll take shit from there."

* * *

Rip

"Ahhhh! Ahhh! Fuck you, nigga! I'm tellin' you that shit ain't got nothin' to do with me!" Loc hollered.

I had half of his mouth taped. I left just enough room so I could hear his punk ass scream, but not enough that he could alert the neighbors. I held the hot skillet with the bubbling grease inside it, stepped to him and pouring some more of the grease down his back. I could hear that shit sizzling. It was cool as hell.

"Ahhhhh! Mutha! Fucka! What do you want from me? I don't know why you doing this to me, Cuz. We supposed to be gangstas, nigga. Family."

I stepped to him again, ready to pour some more of the grease on him. "Look punk, now I told you that somebody snatched up my daughter. She missing in action, and the only mafuckas I know that get down like that is you, and that bitch-ass brim nigga, Looney. Now, I know y'all got this new treaty and the only way it came to be, is because it was decided that I was gone fall back from the family. I don't know what that means entirely, but nigga, I know you a snake. Don't nobody in Vegas trust you, that's including me."

I sat the skillet back onto the hot plate I had plugged up in their basement and added some more lard into it. I watched that shit melt quick as hell. The eye on the hot plate was bright red and I knew that meant hot.

After I set everything down, I took the steak knife that I had grabbed from the top drawer in the kitchen. I stepped to Loc and stabbed it in his shoulder. He jumped back and opened his mouth as wide as the tape would allow him to. A big smile crossed my face.

"Arrrrghhhh! You muthafucka!" He tried to move out of his binds but wasn't nothing moving. That nigga was wrapped up better than a Christmas present.

I pointed the steak knife at his face. "Nigga, most of the licks I done hit, you know about them. All the niggas in Vegas I popped off, you know about them, too. So, if any heat came for me, and a mafucka was talking about hitting yo hand, you the type of nigga that'll sell yo soul for it. So nigga, if you don't know where my daughter at, you definitely know who took her." I took the blade and slowly drug it across his face, slicing and leaving a thin line of blood, which became major the further I slid it across. Every trace of blood I saw, motivated me to go harder. I was missing Bree. I needed her.

"Okay, okay. But this shit ain't got nothing to do with me. It's them punk-ass Pesci's. They got your daughter. You must have killed one of them while you were robbing Kelly. They sent their treasurer to pick up some money from him, and in the process, he was whacked by you. They got that shit on camera. They want your life. That's all I know."

My heart dropped. The first thing that came to my mind was what he had said about a fuckin' camera. I should have known that Kelly's soft ass had security cameras everywhere. Bitch-ass nigga. Then, I thought about how their family got down, and I started to panic and worry for Bree. Their family was known for killing black kids. They didn't really hurt whites, but when it came to our children, they didn't hesitate to kill them. That thought pissed me off.

I walked over to Peaches and knelt in front of her. I put my hand on her thick thigh and squeezed. "Peaches, look at me, because I'm finna ask you something and I really want you to take what I'm going to say into consideration. You hear me, baby?"

She nodded, looking so fucking fine. Keeping shit one hunnit, I was mentally present on the mission, but I couldn't help that every time I looked at this girl, I was feeling some type of way.

Her shirt had rolled up a little bit and it showed off her stomach. There were a few stretch marks across it and I could tell they were from having her children, and I don't know why, but it was just the sexiest thing in the world to me. I feel like women with post-pregnancy bodies are hot. I had to focus 'cuz a nigga was getting side tracked.

104

"Peaches, I know this nigga is triflin', and that he ain't on shit with you and your little men. I know you tired of fucking this fat nigga, and that support ain't what it's supposed to be, so I gotta give you two options, and you only got a few seconds to make up your mind before I take them away and make the decision myself." I stood up and walked over, picking up the duffel bag of cash I had gotten by cleaning out all three of his safes. It had to be about a hundred gees, easily. I took the bag and dropped it by her foot. "Shorty, you got two kids. Kids this bitch nigga don't really give a fuck about, because he don't know the first steps to being a man. I know you tired of him degrading you. I know you tired of him treating you less than a queen. You fight for the boys every single day by any means, don't you?"

She blinked and tears sailed down her cheeks, before nodding her head. "Yes."

"You love them with all of your heart, don't you?"

She was really crying now. "Yes, Rip, I do. I'll do anything for my children."

I pointed at Loc with my head. "And do you think this bitch-ass nigga would?"

She looked at him for a long time with tears falling down her cheeks. Her top lip quivered. Her chest rose and fell. She looked like she was going through an emotional storm.

"Keep in mind how this nigga talk to you, all the things he make you do for them peanuts, and how many times you felt sick on the stomach because you had to sexually please this bitch-ass nigga. The amount of times you cried yourself to sleep. How much time he spends with them. All of it."

She shook her head.

I grabbed her hand and kissed it. "Ma, you are a queen, fuck what dude talking about. You need to know you are a beautiful, black, strong queen, and you don't need no nigga that's gone tear you down." I kissed her hand again. "Now, it's about three or four hundred thousand dollars in this bag right here, and I wanna give it to you because you deserve it. But, there is a dilemma. It's either you kill this nigga and take that money, so you and yo kids can live happily ever after. Or, I gotta kill him on my own, and then unfortunately, the code of the streets says I gotta body you and them as well. I mean, you already know how the game go. I leaned over and kissed her on her forehead. "So, what's it gone be, queen?"

She sniffed snot back into her nose. "I'll kill that nigga with no effort." Tears dripped from her face. "Just tell me how you want it done."

Five minutes later, I had moved her children upstairs. They were still knocked out cold, but I placed two pillowcases apiece over their heads just in case they woke up. I didn't want them seeing my face again. I stood behind Peaches' big ass booty and rubbed my front all on it, just absorbing the feeling.

I grabbed Loc by his dirty ass dreads and pulled his head back.

"Don't do this shit, Peaches. You know I love you, baby. You know I love you, come on now."

I yanked his head back harder. "Now look, baby, this is the line I want you to follow. I want you to slice him from here to here. Now, you gotta really dig into him too, I mean, with all of your might. If you gotta imagine him hurting you or one of your boys, then do it, because it makes killing so much easier. Trust me, but let's go."

Peaches rolled her head around on her shoulders, then took the knife and stabbed it into his neck, causing his blood to spurt up like a geyser. I jumped back a little bit and laughed.

"Nall, you gotta slice him, not stab, like you cutting something."

Loc was shaking in his seat like a mad man, acting like he was having a seizure. I held down his shoulders and pulled his head back again, all the while sniffing up Peaches and loving her lil sweaty scent.

"Oh, I see what you're saying, you mean like this." She took the knife and sliced his throat from one ear to the next, and then from that one to the other, and back again. It got to the point where I stood back and let her do her. I loved how it looked. I had never seen a female kill a dude before, and that shit was cool as hell.

Loc flopped around like a fish, while his blood attacked the air. When she was done, she looked like she'd had a tomato sauce fight with somebody and lost. I gave her every penny of the money, because in my book, she deserved it.

Chapter 12

J.T.

"So what, we're just supposed to babysit this bitch now? I don't understand," Jennifer said, mugging the shit out of Melanie. I could tell she didn't like her right away and I guess I couldn't blame her.

We were watching the news with the sound off. It was showcasing minor details of what had taken place on Melanie's campus.

"Nall, I'm finna get in contact with that nigga, Looney, and we gone make the trade like that. He gone give me Lil' Momma, and then I'm gone give him Melanie. Long as everything go right, it ain't gone be no problems."

"Wait a minute, J.T., because you said no matter what, you weren't going to hurt me. That I was still your little Barbie. I'm holding you to that."

Jennifer frowned. "Barbie?" She sucked her teeth. "Uh, I don't know who you are, or what you think this is, but you're not his Barbie, bitch. You ain't put no work in around him. He already have two Barbies. And for the record, I doubt if any of that shit in your head is real." She rolled her eyes, before her face turned into a mug of pure hatred.

Melanie bounced off the bed and before I could stop her she ran up on Jennifer and boy, why did she do that?

Boop! Bop! Slap! Bop-bop! Slap! Jennifer hit her so many times, they wound up on the floor with Jennifer on top of her, smacking her again and again.

"Bitch, let's get this shit straight right now. Because you don't run shit in here. J.T. belongs to me and my cousin. Not you! You fake-ass Barbie." She punched her in the nose and blood dripped down each of Melanie's cheeks.

"J.T., get this crazy bitch off of me! Help me! She's whoopin' my ass." I sat on the bed for a minute to give Jennifer her respect.

In the streets, a nigga was forbidden to pull another man off another's ass unless he was being jumped. I looked at Jennifer as part of my family, my baby, my equal. It was my duty to let her do her thing. So, I let her fuck Melanie up until she was finished.

She grabbed the girl up by her throat and put her forehead to hers. "Now, you listen to me, because as long as you here, bitch, you fall under me, not J.T. You gon' sit yo semi-pretty ass down and be still. I'm gon' tie them wrists and yo feet up, until it's time to get rid of yo monkey ass." She brushed her hair out of her face. "Keep in mind that you don't mean nothing to me at all. All I care about is my cousin. So, if you try anything, on my soul, I'm killin' you and I will feel nothin' at all. Not a muthafuckin' thing. You got it?"

Melanie nodded her head with blood pouring out of her nose. She looked terrified and all I could do was shake my head.

Jennifer walked over to me and wrapped her arms around my neck, before kissing me on the lips. "I don't know why you calling that bitch a Barbie, but I ain't going for it. All I ask is that you respect me, and not call her that shit while I'm around. Can you do that?"

I pulled her into my arms and gripped that ass, rubbing all over it, before cuffing it the way it needed to be cuffed. "I got you boo, don't even trip. It ain't even that type of party."

She laid her head on my chest and I could see a big smile on her face.

* * *

Lil Momma

"If you do come out here, y'all already know what I want you to do," Tommy said, looking her up and down as he peeked his head through the door. "It's been a long time and that body been calling me." He licked his crusty lips.

Jamie smiled and ran her hands over her hips. "Well, when is Looney supposed to be back? I ain't trying to get caught doing whatever you wanna do. That nigga a kill both of us, you already know that."

Tommy waved her off and looked her up and down once again hungrily. "That nigga on his way to Melanie's school. He gone be gone for a minute. You already know ain't gone take me more than a half-hour to do my thing, we just gotta hurry up. So, come on."

He grabbed her by the arm and yanked her out of the room so fast, she almost fell. After he slammed the door, I waited to see if he was going to apply the lock. When five minutes went past without him doing it, I couldn't stop my heart from pounding in my chest like crazy. I took a second to gather myself before I went and turned the doorknob very slowly.

To my amazement, it turned and then the door opened. I peeked my head out into the long hallway. The floors were wooden. There were about three other closed brown doors leading down the hallway, and at the end of it was the front room, and the door that allowed a person to enter or exit the house.

I could hear Jamie's moaning. She sounded like he was killing her and I knew she had to be putting on a front, because she had already told me his dick was little. So, I applauded her for doing what it took.

I stepped out into the hallway on bare feet. The pink on my little toenails were damn near gone. It was time for a new touch-up. I tiptoed all the way down the hall, until I got to the living room, and saw his big ass on top of her, humping away like crazy. His ass was hairy like a bear's, and there was so much sweat on his back, it looked like he had ran a marathon.

"Huh! Huh! Huh! Yeah, Jamie. This that good shit right here. Girl, you got that snapper."

Jamie had her eyes closed and was probably imagining being anywhere, but where she really was. I could smell their combined sex scents and it made my stomach turn. "Yeah, Tommy. Make me love it, big daddy. Show me how you get down." She moaned and I could tell it was fake as hell.

I shook my head and then continued to creep toward the front of the house. When I got to the kitchen, I ducked down and looked around for a weapon, while they continued to do them.

I knew I had to seize the moment, because when Looney got back, he was going to go ballistic. That's the kind of man he was. So, I looked around frantically, until I saw the knife holder.

It was all wood and looked like it held a full knife set. I grabbed the biggest one immediately, a big ass butcher's knife. It was heavy in my hand and I felt my heart thumping in my chest, as I slowly made my way into the living room.

Tommy had Jamie's thighs on his shoulders, humping his hairy ass forward, plowing into her again and again, while she screamed like he was killing her.

All that noise was getting on my nerves and I didn't care if my life was depending on it, if a nigga wasn't fucking me right, I was not moaning for him. That shit was a slap in the face to me. Not only was the nigga a dud in the sack, now I had to encourage him? Nall, fuck that, it wasn't happening.

I got as close to them as I possibly could, and me and Jamie made eye contact. Her eyes opened so big, I could tell she was about to have a meltdown. I put my finger to my lips and gave her the "hush yo mouth" look.

She closed her eyes and then I stepped forward and raised the big butcher's knife all the way over my head. I took a deep breath, then jumped into the air and brought the knife down with all of my might, right on the bald spot in the back of his head.

The knife forced its way into his skull and got stuck. I pulled it out and slammed it back again, this time a little harder. His blood exploded and shot everywhere. Jamie started to scream. Tommy fell on his back and I saw he was shaking and bleeding out of his eyes. It poured out of them and ran down his cheeks.

I straddled him and brought the knife down into his chest once, and then again and again and again, until his blood was popping up like crazy. Jamie was screaming loudly. "Bitch, shut the fuck up before I kill yo ass."

She squatted and put her hand over her mouth. I could see Tommy's nut leaking out of her pussy. It looked gross, just because I knew whose semen it was.

I flipped him over and went into his pockets, searching for his keys and as soon as I found them, I felt a sigh of relief. I jumped up and grabbed Jamie by the hair. "Come on, you gotta get dressed and we gotta get out of here."

She jumped up and looked at me like she was terrified. "But, you killed him. You stabbed him. He's fucking dead, what are we going to do?" she whimpered as I slung her down the hall toward the bedroom.

Had she not have been J.T.'s sister, I would have killed that bitch with no hesitation. She was acting too weird, like she was ready to keel over. I was worried about her. I seriously considered killing her and telling J.T. that one of Looney's men did it, but I felt I owed him more than that.

When we got into the room, she started getting dressed right away. I didn't know where Looney was keeping my shoes, so I had to go without them for now. I ran back into the living room and flipped Tommy's fat ass over, taking the .9 millimeter off of his waist, before me and Jamie hit it out the front door and jumped into his beat-up Suburban.

* * *

J.T.

"This nigga ain't answering his phone. I wonder what's really good. Time is of the essence," I said, starting to get a little pissed off.

Jennifer shut the bathroom door, where she had left Melanie in the tub with her mouth taped, along with her hands and feet. She walked over to me and kissed my lips. "Baby, don't stress yourself. That nigga gotta answer his phone soon. He's probably being interviewed by the police or something. But, you already know he gone get back to you." She rubbed my chest and then kissed my neck, before biting it with her teeth. "Is there anything that I can do for you?"

Her scent went right up my nose. Damn, it wasn't nothing like the scent of a woman. She smelled feminine and all-natural. Her long hair cascaded over her shoulders, making her look like a goddess. The more I looked at her, the more I wanted some of that body.

She placed her hand between us and gripped my dick, squeezing it in her little hand. "Can I taste you real quick? Maybe that'll help you think more clearly."

Before I could give her my answer, she was sitting down on the bed and pulling me to her by my waistband. My pants were dropped, and she pulled my dick through my boxer's hole, stroking it up and down, before kissing the head and placing it into her mouth.

114

As soon as the heat surrounded him, I groaned into my throat. It felt so good. I stepped onto my tiptoes and slowly went in and out of her mouth, while she made loud nasty noises all over it.

"I love doing this for you, baby. I love the taste of you, and I'll do this anytime you need me too. I'm here to serve you because I see how you get down for me and my cousin." She took me to the back of her throat and pulled me all the way out, kissing the head and looking at it like it was something really special.

It was all I could take. I had to hit that yellow pussy. I felt that beast coming out of me and before I could control myself, I was ripping off her pants, and throwing her panties on the floor, before placing my face between her thighs and sniffing her pussy. I made sure that scent went all the way up my nose, then I attacked her kat like I was a vicious dog.

I sucked on each pussy lip individually, then licked her juices that were pouring out of her, while she moaned at the top of her lungs. I made sure I peeled them lips all the way back, until her clit popped out. As soon as I saw it, I wrapped my lips around it and sucked hard enough to please her, but not enough to throw her off. I knew it was sensitive, so I split the difference.

She got to wriggling around on the bed and trying to get away from me, and I kept pulling her ass back and eating that kat. Then I laid on my back and she straddled me. I held my dick for her and she slid down on it. Her hot hole engulfing me and making me shiver like crazy. It wasn't nothing like the feel of some hot pussy. The way it squeezed your dick and milked you. That feeling was enough to make me remember it anytime a nigga even thought about looking at her the wrong way. I would be quick to body his ass. Trust me, if you put that

Ghost

pussy down the right way, ladies, a nigga would kill for you.

"Ummm shit, J.T. Umm, shit, Daddy, I love this dick so much. I love it so much. I'm yo real Barbie, not that bitch in there. Not that bitch in there, Dadddeeeee!" She started to bounce up and down on me like we were in a rodeo.

She was going crazy and the higher she bounced, the harder she came down, until she was milking me. I had my mouth wide open, just letting her do her. I pulled them big pretty titties out and pulled on her long nipples, sucking them in my mouth, and trailing my tongue across a few of the stretch marks that meant they were connected to a real woman. That shit turned me on like crazy.

"Ahhh! Ahhh! Awwww, sheeiitttt! Here I come agaiiinnnn!" she yelled and really got to bouncing up and down on me and shaking.

That pussy gripped me tighter and tighter. I could smell it in the air. Looking at her sweaty face, and the way her titties bounced up and down, along with the wet marks from where I'd sucked on them, was all too much. I released my nut in globs, all in that womb.

She really acted a fool when she felt that. She gripped my chest and threw her head back and moaned to the ceiling, riding me like a champion. I squeezed that big booty and ran my finger up and down her asshole opening. "You want some of that, Daddy? Huh? Is that what you want? I'll give it all to you."

I flipped her over in the bed, spread her ass cheeks and licked all in between them, while she held them open for me. I put my middle finger into her hole and ran it in and out, before she came to all fours, and spread herself apart. I noted that she was taking her pussy juices and trailing them up to her asshole.

116

"Come on, J.T. Own me, baby. Please. I need you. I just need you to take over my body. Take me away from all of this pain in my mind. Fuck me like you doing it for me and Lil' Momma."

Every word that came out of her mouth had me falling in love with her. She was appealing to that animal in me. Then, it was turning me on, because we had a whole bitch in the bathroom tied up. I could only imagine what was going through her mind in there, but it excited me.

She reached back, took my dick, and lined it up with her ass, and I pushed him home.

Chapter 13

Rip

"Hey, may I take your order?"

I upped the two big .45's and lowered them, until they were pointed right at Michael's head. He was the youngest of the Pesci brothers, we had all went to school together. They were these stuck-up Italians, famous for loan sharking, and taking high-priced stolen cars and switching the VIN numbers on them, so they could resell them for two thirds of the original price.

As far as I knew, I didn't think they were connected to the mob and if they were, I didn't give a fuck. I was on bitness for Bree. "You punk muthafucka, where is my daughter?"

His eyes lowered and then a smile came across his face. "You know you ripped off one too many people. Sometimes, you have to pay up your debts or bad things happen."

I leaned over the counter. *Boom! Boom!* Two shots, one in each kneecap.

"Ahhhh! Are you fucking crazy? They'll have your ass for this, Rip!" He fell onto his side.

I jumped over the counter, just as a big, beefy, Italian mafucka came out of the back, with a dirty apron on and a shotgun in his hand, ready to buss.

As soon as I saw him, I fell on my back, and aimed both cannons. *Boom! Boom! Boom! Boom!* The barrels spit fire at him. Big round holes appeared on his chest before he flew backward and dropped the gun. I got up and kicked it away from him. Taking Michael by the ponytail, I dragged him across the floor.

A pan dropped in the kitchen and I kicked in the swiveling door and looked around. *Boo-wa! Boo-wa!*

Boo-wa! Shots came at me from the bandit that cooked the food. One of his bullets slammed into the cash register and it exploded, right by me. I dropped to the floor.

The shooter must have thought he hit me, because he ran out of the kitchen in search of me and I lit his ass up like it was the Fourth of July.

Boom! Boom! Boom! Smoke rose in the air. He did a dance as each bullet ripped into his flesh at close range, before doing a one-eighty and flying backward.

I stood over him and gave him one more to the face, splashing him. Michael tried to crawl away. *Boom!* One shot right in the ass. He jumped to his feet, forgetting about his shattered kneecaps, and fell down all over again in pain.

"Aww! You son of a bitch. I'm going to make sure they kill you. I'm going to make sure they cut your fucking heart out," he spat as a pool of blood formed around him.

I kicked him in the chest and he slid across the floor. I continued to look around to see if there was anybody else present. I knew Saturday mornings were the days they usually did their major clean-ups to prepare for the night. I wasn't expecting more than two to be present. So, due to the fact that it had been three, I was a little shaken but it wasn't that big of a deal.

I ran around and closed every door in the store and locked them, before snatching Michael up by his body, and slamming him on the metal counter in the big kitchen. I grabbed a meat cleaver, and chopped off two of his fingers at one time, a pinky and his ring finger.

"Arrrgh! My fucking fingers! What is the matter with you, Rip?" He grabbed his wounded hand and held it to his chest.

Sweat poured down his face. His eyes were red and his entire shirt was drenched in blood and sweat. "I ain't got no time to play wit you, muthafucka. Where is my daughter?" I yanked his hand away from him and placed it on the counter.

"Rip, don't do this shit to me, man. We've always been cool. You know I'm just a pizzant, my brothers don't tell me anything. I swear it, buddy."

"Buddy?" I slammed the cleaver down, again and again. Cutting little pieces of his fingers away, until I was down to his knuckles. I slammed the blade into them and it opened up a huge gash in his hand. I left it, ran over to the seasoning station and poured salt all over it.

"Arrrgggh! Arrrghhh!" he screamed with his mouth opened wide.

I know that shit hurt. For you non-killers out there, listen to me. I done fucked over plenty niggas in real life and made 'em submit by pouring salt into the wounds I'd created. That shit is real. Mafuckas fold real quick when you get to torturing they ass like that. Trust me.

I raised the cleaver again and was ready to bring it down on his shoulder, when he started talking more than Wendy Williams.

"She's over in Arbor Hills. It's my father's estate. My brother, Vino, has her. He wants your life, man. Said he never liked you for something you did back in high school. He's going to kill you, Rip. The money you took from Kelly belonged to our family. You're in deep waters. Now, whatever you do, please just let me go. You're already a dead man. Don't make shit worse for yourself and your kid." His eyes got real big.

"Arrgh!"

I brought the cleaver down on his face again and again. I mean, I was ripping it part. It felt like I was chopping up a pumpkin and he kept trying to beg me to stop, but I kept going, imagining a nasty Italian's hand touching my daughter.

I imagined my baby being scared for her life. Wishing I was there to protect her and I wasn't. I hated the Pesci family. I hated any muthafucka that had a hand in hurting my baby girl.

So, I chopped and chopped, until I was slamming the blade into the table, because his face was no longer there.

* * *

J.T.

I kissed Jennifer's perfect toes and placed her leg back onto the bed. She was already snoring lightly. Kissing her on the forehead was my joy, but still in all, I couldn't get Lil' Momma out of my head. I know people gone say it was impossible for me to be smashing Jennifer and worrying about Lil' Momma at the same time, but I was.

I felt like being with Jennifer was the closest I could actually get to Lil Momma. I felt we all had a bond, and though it was three of us, the bond was split evenly in each direction so that nobody got left out.

But, on some real shit, I was missing her like crazy. I thought about her every second of every single day, and it was killing me that I had not found a way to get her back in my arms.

So yeah, I sought refuge in Jennifer, just like she did me. We were both hurting over Lil' Momma, and I feel like the times we were entwined together, we were healed, just for those few moments.

That nigga, Looney, hit my phone at three in the morning, and I damn near broke my neck getting out of the bed. "What's good, nigga? Let me speak to Lil Momma."

"Muthafucka, where my sister at? Don't tell me you ain't got her, because I know you!" I could hear him cursing in the background. "Man, if you kilt my sister over this punk-ass bitch, nigga, I'mma kill your whole family, starting with Jamie's dope-fiend ass."

I clenched my jaw and tried my best to calm down. That nigga was the reason my sister had started doing heroin. He had the same problem and he figured it'd be cute to get her addicted.

I never understood why niggas thought it was smart to get their women doing the same dope they did. All that created was two habits, and if a man was already struggling to handle the monkey on his back, now he had to juggle that, his woman, and her habit. That shit never made sense to me, that's why I really ain't fuck with drugs like that. I didn't need shit controlling me, my temper was bad enough.

"I got shorty and she good. I ain't harm a hair on her head, 'cuz that ain't my style, nigga. All I want is my jewel back."

Looney was quiet for a few seconds. "Aiight, nigga, where you wanna meet up at?"

Before I could even give him an answer, I saw my phone was ringing again from some unknown number. I answered right away. "What's good? Who dis calling J.T.?"

* * *

Lil Momma

"J.T. oh my God! Baby, I got outta there. I escaped. That nigga was doing too much to me and I escaped on his ass. I need you to come and get me, please." I cried into the phone.

I wasn't crying because I was scared. I was crying because I heard his voice, and it immediately broke me down to my lowest emotional point. I loved J.T. with all of my heart and all I wanted to do was get to him, so I could wrap my arms around his neck and have him pick me up.

"Baby, I'm on the phone with that nigga, Looney, right now and he making it seem like he got you with him. He wanna swap Melanie for you, but you telling me that you bounced on his ass?"

I looked over my shoulder at the two, big white dudes that had let us into their trailer. They looked funny and smelled like beer and sweat. Jamie was already having a full-blown conversation with them, like they were all old high school buddies or something.

"Yeah, that nigga was trying to fuck me every single day. He had me doing crazy shit with your sister and everything. We bounced earlier today, and I would have called you earlier, but I had forgot your phone number. You know it's in my phone, so I been sitting here for the last four hours, trying to figure it out."

I saw one of the white dudes put his arm around Jamie, and they all started to laugh. In my opinion, everybody looked too comfortable, and I was nowhere near it. I told J.T. where we was before hanging up the phone and telling him to hurry.

I turned around and looked over the three behind me, before one of the white dudes, with a stomach so big he looked like he'd just ate, came over and tried to hand me a beer. His beard looked like it stank, and it probably did, but I definitely wasn't trying to find out.

"Here you go, little lady. I'm sure you could use a nice cold one, as hot as you are." He licked his lips and I almost threw up in his face.

I gave him a look that should have said I was disgusted by him, but all he did was smile, and rubbed his long beard as if it was the sexiest thing in the world. I caught a whiff of his underarms, and my stomach turned.

"Uh, no, thank you. But, I don't drink at all." I held up my hand and turned my head away from him.

He groaned. "Aw, come on now, little lady. What's one little brew gonna do? Everyone is grown here." He looked me up and down. "You sure are."

I could already see where this was going and I wasn't having it. "Look, me and my sister just gone wait outside for our ride. Thank you for letting us use the phone. When our ride gets here, we'll make sure you're compensated for that. Come on, Jamie, it's time to go."

She uncrossed her legs and started to get up, but the other biker-looking white dude pulled her down and kissed her on the cheek. "Well, I can tell you right now that she ain't ready to go nowhere. Looks like this lady is having a mighty fine time and you're just being a party pooper," he said, squeezing her thigh.

Jamie tried to knock his hand away, but he kept on messing with her. "Hey, maybe you should let me up, so I can go with my sister. We have to stick together, and this isn't right."

He kissed her on the cheek and gave me a look that said he was in full control and would do whatever he wanted to her. I saw his hand squeeze her thigh, as he began to kiss all over her neck loudly.

I was on my way to her, when the other biker got in my way and looked down on me, while pulling his beard. "Hey, why should they be the only ones having fun? I think you and I need to get better acquainted. Create a little white on black." He laughed loudly and tried to pull me into his embrace.

I pushed his ass with what little strength I did have, causing him to fly backwards and land on top of them. "Get the fuck off me, you nasty-ass white man. This ain't that type of party."

When he landed on them, he knocked the beers all over the floor. As he stood up, he stepped on them and beer squirted out of the cans. "You little black bitch. How dare you put your filthy hands on me? Now you're gonna get it." He got to coming at me, looking like a big ass angry bear.

"Yeah, get that bitch, Andy, and I'll take care of this one," the other one said.

I had to be out of my fucking mind. Something told me to not come into a trailer park expecting people to be civil, but Tommy's trash-ass Suburban had broken down about five miles down the road, and this was the first piece of civilization we had seen. I had a weird feeling about it almost right away.

I waited right until this big punk got all the way up on me, thinking he was about to touch me in any way, and I slammed the barrel of Tommy's gun right into his forehead. It must've caught him off guard, because he jumped backward and held his hands in the air with his eyes wide open. "Listen to me, you sick son of a bitch. You and that other sicko over there is gone let me and my sister leave out of here right now. Now, we thank you for allowing us to use the phone, but that's where it ends. You got that?"

He nodded his head up and down and looked like he was terrified. "Hey lady, that sounds cool with me. How about you gals take a few beers with you for the drive home?"

The other biker-looking dude wasn't having any of it. Thank God I looked his way when I did, and thank God J.T. had shown me how to shoot a gun a long time ago, because had he not, I would have been a dead woman along with Jamie.

He pushed her off the couch and flipped it over, leaned down and picked up a big ass shotgun. It was like it all happened in slow motion. He loaded it up with the red-cased bullets, pumped it up and down, then turned it and aimed at me.

Quick thinking told me to save myself, so I pushed Andy

out of my face, and he wound up right in the line of his friend's fire.

Boooom! Boooom!

Two big ass holes formed on his back and I saw blood spurt out his mouth, before he fell to the ground on his knees.

Jamie started to scream so loud, I wanted to slap her ass. I cocked the pistol back, aimed at him and fired three times. *Boom! Boom! Boom!*

The first two bullets missed him, but the third caught him right in the forehead. His head jerked backward, and his eyes trailed upward to the hole in its center, before he dropped to his knees slowly and fell on his face. I lay on my back with the gun smoking, the smell of gunpowder heavily in the air.

Jamie was curled into a ball with her hands over her ears, shaking her head from side to side as if she was in shock.

Chapter 14

J.T.

"Get up, Jennifer," I ordered, smacking her on her ass, as I strapped my bulletproof vest across my chest, and threw a black shirt on over it.

She sat up in the bed, and stretched her arms above her head, yawning as if she was dead tired. She probably was being that we had done the most all night. "What time is it?"

I tied the laces to my Jordans and flipped my pants over them. "It's like three thirty."

She looked around. "Where are you going?"

"Lil Momma just called me. She broke away from that nigga, so now I gotta go and get her. We gotta hurry up."

She immediately shot out of the bed at the mention of Lil' Momma's name. She got dressed quickly while asking me a million questions, it seemed. "When did she call you? How did she sound? Did she say he hurt her at all? How far away is she? Why you didn't wake me up so I could hear her voice too?" She started to cry while trying to get her shoes on her feet. "I miss her so much. She's my heart, and I can't wait to hug her. Fuck, I gotta pee." She ran to the bathroom.

I was trying to figure out how I was gone play Looney's bitch ass. I told the nigga I would meet up with him in the afternoon and I fully intended on doing that. That nigga had to pay for his sins. Not only had he fucked over Lil Momma, but he fucked over my sister and mother. I wanted to teach home boy a lesson, so I was trying to figure shit out in my mind.

Jennifer came out of the bathroom with her hair in a long ponytail. She was fine as hell. I just had to let that be known. "Um, so if we're going to get Lil Momma, and Looney no longer has her, what the fuck are we going to do with that bitch in there?" She pointed over her shoulder with her thumb.

I shook my head. I had forgotten all about Melanie and to be honest with you, I didn't know what I wanted to do with her. I walked toward her. "Go wait for me in the car. I'll be down in the minute."

Jennifer gave me a crazy look. "Hey, are you going to kill her? Because if you are, let me do it for that Barbie shit she was hollering earlier. I still haven't gotten over that."

I had to laugh at that, because after being around me for a little while, I had turned her into a complete savage. When we'd first linked up, she was a pure sweetheart. Now, her heart was as cold as me and Lil Momma's. I liked that. I know that's crazy to say, but I did. "Nall, I ain't gone kill her because we gone still use her as bait. I just wanna get some shit straight with her before we take her outside again."

Jennifer looked me over closely, and then nodded. She kissed me on the cheek, and then the lips. "Don't be hollering that Barbie shit though. That will get that bitch fucked up." She walked out of the room, after picking up the bag of money.

I took a deep breath and opened the bathroom door, moving back the shower curtain. Melanie lay with her head against the rim of the tub, her eyes closed and she was even snoring a little bit through her nose. I moved her hair out of her face.

"Melanie. Melanie." I nudged her shoulder just a little bit.

She jerked in a frenzy and then opened her eyes. I could hear her trying to talk to me through the duct tape around her mouth.

"Look, your brother wanna meet up, and we gone do this swap this afternoon. Long as he ain't on no bullshit, everything should go smoothly. But, I'm finna move you again, so I don't need you making no scene, do you understand that?"

She nodded her head, and blinked tears. I stripped the tape away from her mouth. She took a deep breath. "J.T., my nose is stopped up. I been trying to breathe for the last few hours with difficulty. Geez, man, are you trying to kill me?"

I picked her up out of the tub and dusted her clothes off. She smelled like sweat and stale perfume. "I didn't know that. You already know if I ain't gotta hurt you, I won't. Now, I can't speak for everybody though."

"You talking about that pretty chick you got wit you, huh?" she asked as I untied her hands.

"You just don't give her a reason to handle her business because she ain't gone hesitate. You hear me?"

She nodded. "Uh-ohh."

I frowned. "Uh-oh what?"

She looked down and bit into her bottom lip nervously. "I think it's that time of the month, and I'm not prepared."

I saw the red stains in the front of her pants and along her inner thighs. "Don't even trip. I'll make sure you're good. For now, go ahead and take a quick shower, and I'll find you a tampon."

* * *

Rip

I waited until he closed the door and started the car, before hopping up and jamming the barrel of my .44 Desert Eagle into the back of his head, cocking the hammer. I could feel his entire body tense up. "I don't

131

have much money. Just what's in my wallet. You can have it all, just please don't kill me. I have a wife and two small boys."

"You think I give a fuck about yo kids, nigga! Huh?" I asked through clenched teeth. This was Sammy, Vino's right-hand man. Anything Vino did, Sammy was sure to know about, there was no exception to the rule. It had been that way since high school.

He started to stutter. "I. I. I. I don't. I don't understand. who are you? What's your deal with me and my family? I'm Catholic. God-fearing."

That was another pet peeve of mine. I hated when a mafucka was on the other end of the gun, and tried to either turn pussy, or turn religious. Neither one of them worked in my book, and it usually ended with me killing them, or fucking them up so bad, they never used that strategy again.

"Sammy, I need to know why Vino took my daughter, and I need you to tell me if she's really up at Arbor Hills?"

"Rip. Man, I swear I didn't have anything to do with your daughter being taken. I didn't make the call. I was just following orders from up top. It's nothing personal, just unfortunate business. I swear, I…" He paused and looked out of the window and seemed to get sick.

I looked over his shoulder, and saw his wife coming to the car, holding the hands of his twin boys. They looked to be about five years old now, the same age as Bree. I felt my heart become heavy all over again. I was thankful after all these years Sammy still went to the same church, at the same time, every Sunday. Sometimes a person's normal routine is what could get them kilt.

"Hey look, Rip, please don't involve my family in this shit, man. Please. Me and my wife are already on

132

shaky ground, then my boys are fragile, man. If they see you waving a gun in their faces, they are going to freak out and lose their minds. They will never recover. Come on, man, let me wave her away."

He sounded like a whiny four-year-old and it made me want to pop his ass. I poked him in the back of the head more forcefully. "Sammy, if you tip them off, I'mma splatter yo shit all over the interiors of this Benz. You see all this leather? All this gone have your brains splattered on it, then I'm gone kill them too. Now, be still and act normal."

He nodded his head. "Just ain't fair, man. I never liked to screw with families. Even the bosses in the old world didn't allow it."

"Yeah, well, Vino crossed the line, and now all you shiesty muthafuckas gotta pay."

His wife waltzed to the car and opened the passenger's door. "That was just a great message today, honey. I feel so joyful. I can't wait until we get home and I cook us a nice meal. Then, we can sit around the table as a family, before you turn on that Raiders' game." She popped the lock in the back and opened the door.

I was on the floor, with the gun already pointed toward the door I knew she would open. I just prayed when she saw me she didn't scream, because if she did, I was gone have to kill all of them real fast and get up out of there. I was on a real rich and racist side of town called Bensonhurst. It was completely segregated, and I felt it was where the snobbiest people on earth lived.

Before she saw me, both of her sons jumped into the back seat of the car and climbed right past me, like they didn't even see me. That blew my mind back, because it was impossible for them not to. I was right there on the floor, they literally had to brush up against me just to take their seats. She closed the door. "Be sure to put your seat belts on, before you turn on those tablets. Am I making myself clear?"

They didn't say a word, because I had one finger to my lips, and the gun pointing from one kid to the next. I wasn't into killing children, but like I said before, it was a part of the game.

She closed her door and as soon as she did, I jumped up and wrapped my arm around her neck. "Listen to me, bitch. Your husband and I got some business to take care of, and as long as you cooperate, the business will stay between me and him, and not you and your children. Now, he gon' follow my commands and take this car where I tell him to, do you understand me so far? Nod your head if you do."

She nodded. I looked out of the window and saw more people coming out of the church, they stopped and hugged each other and seemed as if they were engaging in conversation.

Sammy's wife, Beverly, slowly started to shake as if she were scared out of her mind.

"Get out of this parking lot and drive until I tell you to pull over. You do anything stupid, it's gonna piss me all the way off."

"Daddy, are we in trouble?" one of the twins beside me asked.

"No, son, we're okay. That's just Daddy's friend and we're playing a game right now. Sit back and play on your tablet, until I tell you it's your turn. Okay?"

"Okaaay." He sat back and I could hear his tablet loud and clear.

"But, I'm scared," said the other one. "I think this man is scary-looking, and what is he doing to my mommy? I'm so scared right now."

"Samuel, sit back, don't make me tell you or your brother again. Do you guys want spankings?"

"Noooo," they answered in unison.

134

I could hear Beverly whimpering underneath me. I loosened my hold on her neck. I wasn't trying to choke her out or nothing. But, I also couldn't afford for her to jump out of the car, run and go get any help.

The sun was shining through the windows brightly. It was ridiculously hot outside, humid and everything. We drove for about twenty minutes and I was glad there weren't any police in sight, which was odd for Bensonhurst.

After we shook that side of town, I made him take us to Woodlawn, which was a big wooded area were most people went camping. I needed to get away from civilization, so I could get some answers out of him.

* * *

Lil Momma

"How can you just kill people so easily? It's like it's not affecting you at all, and here I am ready to freak out. That's two dead people right there." Jamie sounded like she was getting hysterical.

"Girl, would you shut up." I demanded, mugging her like she had lost her damn mind.

She had been going on and on about them two dead bikers. I was over it. Life had to move on. I finished washing out the big bowl in the sink, dried it out, and poured the rest of the Fruit Loops inside of it. Thankfully, they had milk, because I was hungry as hell. I had refused to eat anything Looney or his people tried to bring me, over the last three days, so I was starving and feeling a little dizzy.

"And you're about to eat? Really? With them right over there like that?" Her eyes were open so wide, there was lines all across her forehead. She looked shocked and amazed. "Oh, hell nall. My brother done fucked you up. You're nuts. I can't believe this bitch is about to eat some fucking cereal while two corpses are on the floor."

By the time she finished that sentence, I was crunching loudly with my eyes closed. Them Fruit Loops was bomb. I promise you, I ain't lying.

Jamie came over and stood by me when one of the bikers jerked on the floor. She even let out a little yelp. "What the fuck was that?"

I was still crunching away. I spooned more cereal into my mouth and drank some of the milk by tilting the bowl. "Girl, would you just chill? J.T. said that most dead bodies do that, it's just their nerves shutting down."

She looked at me and bucked her eyes open even wider. "Well, I think it's time we get out of here, because I'm freaking out. I can't take this shit no more." She was all behind my chair like I was gone save her if a boogey man came. I kept on crunching and shaking my head.

There was the sound of at least two motorcycles in the distance, but the noise kept on getting louder and louder until it sounded like they were literally inside the house. The engines turned off, and then there was the sound of boots on gravel, before the pounding on the door.

I tilted my bowl of cereal and drank as much of the milk as I possibly could, while the cereal still inside of it brushed up against my lip, all soggy and whatnot. I took the bowl and dumped it out, turned on the faucet, and rinsed the bowl out real well to hopefully destroy any traces of my DNA.

Now, I know you're saying, who in the hell kills two people, and doesn't leave right away? Well, the answer is my stupid ass. I was so hungry. I had to put something in my stomach before I fainted, seriously.

There was more beating on the door. "Hey, open the damn door, man. We're tired, been on the road all night," came a voice from the other side of the door.

"What are we going to do, Lil Momma? What the fuck are we going to do?" Jamie asked, shaking my shoulders like she was crazy.

After my head bounced around on my neck a few times, I had to knock her hands away from me. "Chill, bitch, you just sit right there, I got this. Don't move until I say run. You hear me?"

She looked like she was very unsure, but slowly nodded her head anyway.

* * *

Rip

"Come on, Sammy, you're embarrassing yourself in front of yo family. Now, put you hand back up there and take this shit like a man. Now, nigga!"

"Please, man. Don't make me do this. Please, just let me go, Rip. We didn't have anything to do with your kid being taken. I was against it."

"Did you stop them from taking her, or did you help?"

I felt the sun beaming down on my forehead, causing me to sweat profusely. I was even sweating under my arms, and I really hated that feeling.

Tears soaked Sammy's entire face. It looked like he'd been hit with a water balloon. "I can't control what they do up top, man. You know I can't control them. If I don't listen to them, I'm done for. So yeah, I helped, but I never hurt her, and I was against it from the beginning. It was all Vino's idea. He called the shots."

I nodded. "Sammy, put your hand up there or I'm killing him." I yanked open the door and pulled out one of his twins.

"Dad! Help!"

I grabbed the little boy by his neck and held him in the air, with the gun to his forehead. I wasn't into killing kids, but the more I thought about them fucking over Bree, the colder my heart got. "Put yo muthafucking hand up there, this is yo last warning."

Sammy placed his hand into the space where the trunk was supposed to close. "Please, don't do this, Rip. I respect you, man. I always have."

Whoom! It came down so fast that he had to look down at his smashed hand, before he hollered out so loud, birds flew from the top of the trees they were perched in.

"Ahhhhhhhh! Ahhhhhhh!" Sammy hollered and fell to his knees. His hand still stuck inside of the car's trunk.

Beverly ran out of the passenger's seat, holding her other son by the back of his head. He cried into her chest, and she bounced him up and down. "This isn't right! This isn't right, you brute! Leave our family alone." She put her son down and came at me, swinging wildly.

I was shocked. I dropped the other little boy, ducked one of her punches and swept my leg under hers, dropping her to the tall grass. "Bitch, chill. I told you, this ain't got shit to do with you."

"Ahhhhhh! Ahhhhh! Son of a bitch, this shit hurts!" Sammy continued to holler behind me.

Beverly bounced up and came at me again with her fist, swinging like she was out of her mind. I noticed she had her eyes closed and everything. I had a trick for her ass.

Chapter 15

Lil Momma

"Come on in, gentlemen, and make yourselves at home. We were told you'd be arriving," I said, sounding like the best escort in the world probably.

The big fat biker looked me up and down and scratched his bald head. "Say, who the hell are you, and when we did start screwing black whores?"

That comment made me wanna pop his ass right away with his disrespectful ass. And, to top it off, he smelled like sweat and ass. How a mafucka gonna be stank *and* disrespectful? If I thought the other two bikers stunk, well, they had nothing on him.

Another biker that was just as fat as the one in my face moved him aside and looked me up and down with lust in his eyes.

"Well, what do we have here? Looks to be some of that good old plantation pussy. Gosh darn it, my requests are finally being heard around here." He grabbed my hand and kissed it.

I wanted to throw up on his dirty ass black boots. Ugh, I was disgusted. "Y'all, come on in, fellas, so we can get to know each other."

The sun was doing a number on me. I looked past their shoulders and didn't see anybody else out. I was thankful for that.

"Don't mind if I do," the second one said and stepped into the trailer.

As soon as he went in, the other one bumped me slightly and went in behind him. He left a trail of funk behind him. Uh, it was horrible.

"Well, we got ourselves a whole 'nother one in here. Think it's about to be a party."

As soon as the second one stepped in, he snatched Jamie up right away, and started kissing all over her. I mean, he was super rough. I didn't think that was cool at all. When the first funky dude took off his shirt, and started to make his way over to me, I made my mind up right away.

I took the pistol out of the small of my back and held it straight out, leveled at his chest. He kept on walking forward like it was a game. I smiled at that. *Boom! Boom! Boom!*

When the bullets hit him, his body jerked but he kept on coming forward, until he fell on top of me and wrapped his hand around my neck, choking the shit out of me. I couldn't breathe, nor could I move.

Boom! Boom! Boom!

His body leaped in the air, and then he rolled to his side. I heard Jamie scream. I pushed the big funky man off of me and stood up with the gun aimed at the other biker. He had Jamie in front of him with a knife to her neck.

"I don't know what we've walked into, but I ain't going out like that. You're gonna drop that gun and kick it over to me, or your sister here is dead." He slowly sliced a little bit of her neck until she started to bleed.

I felt myself getting ready to panic. I didn't know what to do. On the one hand, I didn't really give a fuck about Jamie like that, but I loved her brother and I knew her death would shatter him. But then, on the other hand, this biker could possibly kill me and Jamie and that wouldn't help nobody, so I was stuck.

"Give me the gun, bitch!" He slowly walked backward as if he were trying to slip out of the door. I had visions on blowing him away, and him flying out of the window that was behind him. I could see the blood oozing out of Jamie's neck. She looked terrified. Tears sailed down her cheeks and I started to feel some type of way.

He jerked her. "Lady, I'm not playing with you, either you drop that gun or I'm killing this bitch. Do it now! Nooow!" he hollered.

I saw him cutting deeper into her neck and a tear dropped from my eye, because I was finna let her ass die. I definitely wasn't risking him killing me too.

"Okay, hey stop. Here, just take the gun," I said, hoping he would lower the knife so I could get a shot at him.

He shook his head. "I'm not stupid, nigger bitch. You drop it by your feet and kick it over here, or she dies, and then I'll go. But, I'm taking one of you with me. You know what, fuck this!" He took the knife and looked like he was about to saw her head off. I couldn't get a clear shot at him. No matter what I wasn't secure of my aim, so I was going to sit there and wait for him to kill her and finish his ass off. I saw the blade moving in slow motion.

Boom! Boom! Boom! Boom! Tisssshh! Boom! Boom! The trailer felt like it was rocking back and forth as the window on the door shattered, and the big biker was hit at least six times. He threw Jamie to the floor, and she covered her head and started screaming loudly. I dropped to the ground and covered my head as well. I didn't know where the shots were coming from, but I knew I was going to die.

* * *

Rip

I grabbed her by her neck and slammed her as hard as I possibly could on the top of the trunk, just so it could smash down harder on her husband's hand.

"Ahhhhhh! Ahhhhh! Please, make it stop!" he hollered, with sweat pouring down his face. His wife jumped off of the car and held up her guards up.

"I'm not afraid of you. You want to kill my family? Well, you have to go through me, and it's not going to be easy." She ran at me full speed.

I frowned. I was tired of playing with her ass. So, as soon as she got in front of me, I punched her like I would a nigga. I rocked her ass then crouched down, scooped her up and slammed her on her back so hard, she bounced up from the grass and turned on her side in pain.

I fell on the ground beside her, wrapped my legs around her waist and put her in the sleeper hold, while her two sons started fucking me up, crying at the same time.

"Ack! Ack! Ack! Let me. Ack! Ack!" I could feel her fight going away. She slowly stopped struggling, and only when she fully stopped did I get up, take the two little boys and clock their heads together. They knocked right out, fell on the grass with their mouths open.

I walked over to Sammy and punched him in the jaw. "I want an address, Sammy. Nall, better yet, you gone set up a meeting with Vino, and we're going to get my daughter back, together. Do you hear me?"

He shook his head. "He'll never fall for it. He and I aren't on the best terms right now, because of some broad from our old school. You wanna get to Vino, you get to her first, it's the only way."

I frowned. "What's her name?" I grabbed him by the throat.

I think it was the sun, getting me more and more irritated. I hated intense heat. I was sweating everywhere and dealing with dude's family was exhausting within itself. I wanted to be done with it already.

He shook his head real hard. "Oh, hell no. I'm not going for that. I give you that broad's name, and you don't need me no more. Then what's going to happen to me and my family? Huh, Rip?"

I punched him straight in the eye and took a step back, leaped forward and another blow right into the same eye. You should have heard how loud he hollered. So loud, he woke up his twins. "Stop playing wit me, Sammy, and give me her name or shit finna get real."

He dropped to his knees, and I opened the trunk so his hand could fall out of it. He wound up on his back, crying like a big ass baby. "Why do we have to go this route, Rip? All I want to do is be able to leave here with my family, man. I don't want any problems with you."

I stood over him with the pistol directly at his forehead.

"What's her name, Sammy? I ain't gone ask you this shit again."

He looked up to me for a brief moment, as tears rolling

rolled down his cheeks. "Aerial. Her name is Aerial, and she works out of the Bunny Ranch. She stays at those condos over on Allied Drive. She drives a pink Corvette. The license plates say, 'Spoiled'. Now please, just let us go, Rip. I swear, I won't say nothing. You can take my word for it."

Like I said before, I wasn't really a big fan of killing women and children, unless the game called for it. I felt like that was one of the things men had to consider when they left the house every day. They had to consider their families before they jumped into whatever it was they were going to do, because more often than not, the streets never stayed in the streets. Most times, whatever you did in them followed you back home and allowed your family to become a part of them. That was just the way it was. So yeah, I felt some type of way about killing females and kids, but when it came to making sure my own child was safe and sound, I knew I had to do what I had to do.

Boom! Boom! Boom! The bullets ripped Sammy's face apart, while his body jumped off the ground again and again. He fell back with eyes wide open.

His wife was just starting to awaken. *Boom! Boom!* Two shots to her temple, her blood shot across my face and I wiped it off with the back of my hand. She turned on her side, as the juices leaked out of her. It was like a million flies started to land on her right away. I found that odd and a little creepy.

Boom! Boom! Two bullets to one of the twin's faces, he sat all the way up and then fell backward, with his arms hugging himself. I tried to think about other things, and not the fact that I had just bodied a little kid. The game was cold at times, and I had to do what I had to do.

The other got up and took off running. "No! No! You can't shoot me, Mister. I'm sorry." He was trying to run so fast that he kept on falling, because he was looking back at me over his shoulder to try and see where I was.

Boom! The bullet missed, and he still ducked down and kept on running in the tall grass. I was already hot as hell and I really didn't feel like going through all of that. *Boom! Boom!* Damn, my aim sucked. I missed and his little ass kept on running. It looked like he was about fifty yards in front of me. *Boom!* He kept running.

Finally, I knelt and closed one eye, took aim and fired. *Boom!* Another miss, now the little boy had to be about a hundred yards in front of me and still running. The sun got hotter and the humidity seemed to rise. I could barely breathe, and I was sticky. *Boom! Boom! Boom! Boom! Boom!* I fired, running in his direction.

Click. Click. Click. Click. "Fuck!" I was out of bullets and his little ass was still running full speed. I took off behind him with the gun still in my hand, running like my life was depended on it.

The further we got into the woods, the taller the grass got, then came the trees. There were so many of them, at times I couldn't see where he was, and even though the trees provided shade, it did nothing for the humidity. It felt like I was in an oven.

Up ahead, I saw him try and jump over a big log, trip and fall flat on his face. " Mommy! Help me, Mommy! Help!"

When I got to him, he was sitting on his backside crying, with a long cut on his face. His face was red and he looked so vulnerable. I felt some type of way almost immediately.

"Please don't hurt me, Mister. I need my mommy. I got a scratch right here."

I shook my head. I couldn't allow myself to think, or process any form of empathetic emotion, I just had to handle business.

I snatched him up and wrapped my arm around his neck, with his back to my chest and squeezed with all of my might, choking him harder and harder. The whole time, the only person I was thinking about was my daughter. I imagined the filthy men touching her in any way and it allowed me to do what I had to do. By the time I dropped him, he was stiff as a board.

* * *

J.T.

Boom! Boom! Boom! Boom! I saw my bullets knock holes into that fat biker. I was waiting the whole time for him to get closer to the door, so I could hit his chest and stomach. I had a perfect view of him through the window. My only worry was of my bullets going through him and hitting my sister, but I figured he was fat enough, and that had a small chance of happening.

I had originally pulled up and got out of my car, with intentions of knocking on the trailer door, but when I heard all of the commotion inside, something told me to crouch down and look through the window, and I was glad that I did.

As soon as dude's bitch ass fell, I took my shoulder and bussed through the door. Jennifer was right behind me with her pistol out, ready for action.

"Ahhh! Ahh!" Jamie screamed at the top of her lungs. That girl had one of those screams that literally hurt your ears.

"Jamie, shut yo ass up! It's me, man! Damn," I said, irritated as hell.

Lil Momma jumped up and ran right into my arms, hugging me like she hadn't seen me in years. "I knew you was gone come for me, J.T. I knew you had my back, baby." She stood on her tippy toes and kissed me on the lips, before we got to going crazy with our tongues. I mean, we were sucking, licking, and smacking all over each other loudly. It got to getting so good, I scooped her ass in the air and she wrapped her legs around me, us still going at it.

"Okay, okay. Look, let me hug my cousin too, then we gotta get out of here," Jennifer said, obviously feeling left out.

I put Lil Momma down and she ran and wrapped her arms around Jennifer's neck and kissed her on the lips. They held each other for a long time. "I missed you, babe."

"Me too. Shit ain't been the same without you, Lil Momma. How is your shoulder?" She took a step back and looked her in the eyes.

146

"I'm good. It don't bother me at all no more." She smiled and pulled her into an embrace, before kissing her again.

"Awright, let's get the fuck out of here. That was plenty shooting, so I know somebody heard." As soon as I said that, I saw two police squad cars roll into the trailer park, and park in front of one of the trailers about fifty yards down.

"Let's go, y'all."

Lil Momma went in front of me and grabbed Jennifer's hand. "Oh shit, they looking over here. We gotta get to that car or we finna be in trouble."

They put some pep in their steps, while I grabbed Jamie and made her walk in front of me. "Lil Momma's crazy now. I don't know what you did to that girl, but she ain't got no sense no more."

"Jamie, just walk, girl," I said, irritated.

As soon as we got outside, three police officers looked over at us. I watched the girls file into the car, before one of the officers held up a hand, and started walking our way.

"Excuse me, sir, if I could just speak to you for a moment," he began.

"Who the fuck is this bitch, J.T.?" Lil Momma asked when she saw Melanie. I already knew that was coming, but I ain't have time to get into all of that in that moment.

"Lil Momma, just get into the car. I'll explain all of that shit to you in a minute."

"Don't worry, girl, I'll tell you. It's a long story though, well, not really," Jennifer began.

Now, all three officers were looking in our direction, and the first one started to jog toward us with his hand by his right side. Then, his pistol was drawn. "Freeze, I need you to step away from the vehicle. Now!"

"Y'all duck down!" I knelt and fired three times.
Boom! Boom! Boom!

I don't know if all three hit him, but he flew
backward and wound up on his side, laying still. That's
when the gunfire erupted. The other two officers got to
bussing so much, it shattered our front windshield.

I jumped in the car and stepped on the gas,
throwing it into drive with the back tires spinning wildly.
The girls were screaming and I could barely hear myself
think.

Boom! Boom! boom! Tink! Tink! Boom! The
officers' bullets were relentless. One of them tried to be a
hero. He came and jumped in front of the car as I was
pulling out of the trailer park, and I hit his ass full-on. So
hard, he flew in the air and came down with a thud,
unmoving.

The other officer ran to his aid. I noted he knelt
down beside him and started to check him over. Then,
our car just died. I mean I don't know what happened. All
of a sudden, it shut off and came to a slow roll, before
stopping altogether. I could hear the girls panicking.

"What the fuck are you doing, J.T.?" asked Lil
Momma.

"Fuck, did the car just die?" asked Jennifer.

"Aw Lawd, we going to jail. Lawd knows I'm too
young for this shit," whined Jamie.

"Shut up!" we yelled at her.

I jumped out of the car and took off running right
away. I knew I didn't have any time to waste. By the time
the police officer looked up at me, I was standing over
him with my gun out.

Chapter 16

J.T.

Boom! Boom! Boom! His brains flew out the back of his head. I stood over him and let loose two more shots that ate away his face. "That's for Tamir Rice and Mike Brown. Solidarity, muthafucka!

I didn't know who had seen me in the other trailers, but I imagined a few people had. I didn't have time to go and kick in doors, just to kill witnesses. We had to get out of there. So, after I stripped both officers of their weapons, I loaded into one of the squad cars, and pulled up alongside my girls. They jumped in and I stormed away.

* * *

Rip

"Do you like that, Daddy? You like when I put all of this ass into your lap like this?" the stripper asked, twirling her waist.

I had my hands on her waist, letting her slowly give me a lap dance. It was two days after I had bodied Sammy and his whole family. I had to get that grief off of my chest, get a little sleep, before I headed out and continued the mission of finding my daughter.

I had to pay three hundred dollars up front, just to get into the Bunny Ranch. Then, they allowed me to choose from a whole collection of hoez, and I ain't calling the females out their names. Nall, that's what they were, straight hoez. They were employed at the Bunny Ranch for one specific purpose, and that was to sell pussy.

Ghost

I picked a lil older, dark-skinned chick that looked like she had been around for a minute. I figured she was on her way out. The other females on the menu were so fine, and she was just mediocre. I figured she had probably been with the company since the beginning and would have the lowdown on everybody. Then, due to the fact that she was older, they would be trying to slowly push her out, one way or the other. That would cause anybody to become bitter, and I was praying she was exactly that.

"Umm, yeah. I like this body. I can't believe you was still on the menu. Ain't none of them other broads out there got nothing on you."

She popped her ass a little harder and turned her face to the side and smiled. "You think so?"

I shook my head. "Nall, as soon as I seen you, I already knew I was willing to pay whatever, just to get you on top of me. I'm glad I picked you too."

She made this noise deep within her throat that told me she was flattered. "You have no idea how much I needed to hear that today. I been feeling so down lately. "

I grabbed her waist with both hands and turned her around, so she was facing me. "I mean, we got this room for two hours, why don't we get to know each other, before we get down and dirty? I'm cool with it, if you is."

She took her thumb and rubbed my face. "You're so young and handsome. What are you doing in a place like this?"

I smiled and shrugged my shoulders. "I produce music, and I got a lot of money. I just wanted to have some 'me time', without all the strings attached. Sometimes that world gets the better of you, know what I mean?"

She nodded. "But, you're so fine though. I can't imagine anybody that looks like you being here." She rubbed my face, looking it over closely.

"You just as fine. I mean, look at you. You could be in movies or something. I'd definitely watch it if you were in it." I rubbed her face and kissed her on the cheek.

She blushed, and blinked a few times, before shaking her head. "You better stop that. I don't know why people think that just because we're in this sex industry, we don't have regular feelings, because we do. All this shit you saying to me is affecting me, I'm so fragile right now." She lowered her head.

I rubbed her cheek and moved to the side of the bed so she could sit right beside me. I put my arm around her shoulder, and she laid her head on my chest. I liked that she was so small too. "You wanna talk about it?"

She took a deep breath and exhaled. "I probably shouldn't, as much as I need to. I'm not gone weigh you down like that."

She started messing with the button on my shirt. I could tell she had something heavy on her mind, and I had to find out what it was, so I could get the information I needed from her in regards to Aerial.

"I'll tell you what. If I can guess what's going on, then you have to tell me. But, if I'm wrong, then you don't have to, and you can treat me like a regular customer. How does that sound?" I kissed her cheeks and noted she smelled like Chanel No.5. I always loved that fragrance.

She nodded her head and turned to look me in the eye. "Okay, you're on."

"Are you tired of the way you're being treated around here?"

"Okay, that's somewhat of the issue, but not quite." She gave me a look that said she was hoping I figured it out, because she really wanted to talk about it.

"Are you tired of how everybody gangs up on you around here? They treat you like an outsider just because you're a little older than them, and clearly two times more sexy."

She smiled. "It's not only that, but I was here when this company first came into existence. I have been bussing my ass here ever since I left high school, and I have never complained about anything. But, now that he's recruiting all of these younger airheads, I'm all of a sudden an acquired taste. Vintage, and all of these other hurtful terms they use in regards to me. I don't like it. It makes me feel like shit, and I'm only human." She blinked as tears slid down her cheeks. She looked heartbroken and that made me feel some type of way.

I put my arm around her neck. "I want you to just speak your mind and just tell me whatever's on your heart. Don't think of me as anybody else other than a listener. You hear me?" I tilted her chin upward and it was the first time I noticed she had in fake, blue contact lenses.

She nodded. "Well, I helped Jerry build this company. He started with just me and one other girl. I used my financial aid refund money, gave him the residual three times, that was nearly twenty thousand dollars, and Gia did the same thing. Back then, he was so sweet. Always treating us like queens and making sure we were well respected in this town. But, as soon as things started to take off for him, I was kicked to the curb and made out to be some regular whore that worked in his establishment. I mean, it's not fair and what's screwed up is that I feel the only reason I am being treated this way, is because I'm a black girl in a Caucasian-dominated field."

She lowered her head and put her hands over her face, sobbing. I held her more firmly and kissed her on the ear, placing my lips right against the right one. "What can I do to help you? Just name it and I'll try my best to make it happen for you. I got a lot of friends in high places."

She shrugged her shoulders. "I'm all washed up now. I don't know what I want to do with myself. I guess if I had some form of cash tucked away I would be alright, but I've been so dependent on him, I wasn't even smart enough to do that. I'm so stupid." Now she was really crying and sobbing.

I had to find a way to make all of this beneficial for me. I know that sounds selfish, but the only way I was gone be able to get my daughter back was if I moved very strategically. I needed this broad.

I wanted to go straight to Aerial, but to me that would have been a dumb move. There was nothing I could have said to that woman that would have made her rollover on Vino on the first day. To even think shit would have been that easy would have been naïve of me. I was better than that. So, I had to find a way to use her to get to Aerial. And Aerial would lead me to Vino.

She sniffed. "I'm sorry. I'm not usually this emotional. It's just that I've been going through so much over the last few years, and now it's all starting to come down on me at once. I feel so lost and so alone. I don't have any family that loves me. The last person who cared about me recently passed away two months ago. So, if I leave Jerry, than I might as well go and live on Skid Row." She broke down again and I rubbed her back.

I really did feel sorry for her, and I wanted to help her out as much as I could. I know that sound crazy, but even though I killed mafuckas and got down like I did, I was still a person at the end of the day with human feelings. I didn't like seeing women break down, or struggle, and if I could help them in any way at all, I almost always did. That's just the kind of man I was. It didn't take away from my gangsta either, so don't get it twisted.

"What if I told you that I want to help you by putting a nice amount of cash in your hands, what would you say to that?" I brushed her hair out of her face and kissed her on the cheek. It was soft and she smelled so damn good.

She blinked, and a little snot came out of her nose. She turned away from me, reached and grabbed a Kleenex, blowing it. After blowing her nose out, and wiping it, she turned back to me and smiled. "Why do you want to help me so bad? Do I sound and look that pathetic?"

I rubbed her cheek with my thumb. "Nall, it ain't that, but you do seem real vulnerable. I wanna help you, and I know that I can. It ain't gone be no sweat off of my brow either." I looked her straight in the eyes. She was starting to get prettier to me. I don't know why vulnerable women always had that effect on me.

She nodded, "Okay, but I've been in this game a long time, and I know that nothing comes free, so what am I going to have to do?"

"Do you know Aerial that works here?"

She made a disgusted face. "Yeah, what about her?" She said this so dryly, I could tell there was bad blood between them.

"Tell me something about her? I guess you can start with why you guys don't get along?"

She shot up, and looked at me angrily. "Is that what this is all about? Did that bitch send you in here to make peace with me? Because I ain't going. I hate her fucking guts. She's a backstabbing whore and I wish she were dead. In fact, I wished I had enough guts to kill her, because I would do it myself with no hesitation." Her chest started heaving up and down.

I could see that she was pissed. Her brown complexion had turned a shade of red. There was even a little sweat along the edges of her forehead and the room was air conditioned.

I pulled her lil sexy ass down and wrapped her into my arms, laughing. "Chill, ma. I don't fuck with her like that, but I need to get to her so I can handle some business with one of her male friends that crossed me."

She looked at me from the corners of her eye. "You gotta be talking about Vino. Am I right?"

Now, I really didn't want to confirm or deny because who was to say that she wouldn't go right and get in touch with Vino as soon as I left her presence. I didn't know her from Adam, and even though I felt like I was reading her pretty good, I was still in position to chance it. "Let's just say I am. Would you be willing to earn twenty gees to get me in his presence and under the banner of sex and celebration?"

Her eyes were opened super wide now. "Twenty thousand? Twenty fucking thousand dollars? Are you kidding me? For twenty thousand dollars, I'd kill Aerial and Vino for you myself." She paced in front of me. "But first, I need to know what I'm getting into. Would I be in any danger?

I shook my head. "As long as everything goes right, you would be perfectly safe." Now, to be honest, I didn't know if she was going to be or not, but obviously I couldn't tell her that. All I saw was me getting closer to my daughter. I was getting anxious. I missed her so bad. She was my everything.

"Well, if you can assure me of that, then I can set some shit up. Vino's having a birthday party at his mansion out on Monona Road, and I've already been invited with a plus-one. If you fix yourself up a little bit, I'm sure I could bring you and we can go from there. In

155

the meantime, there are some other kinks that I need to work out, but all you have to do is leave them to me and if this goes through, I want Aerial knocked off. You do that, and we have a deal. "

I pulled her into my embrace. "I got you, and I'mma make sure you're forever straight. Now, let's sit down and talk for a minute, so we can get a full understanding."

"You gone give me some of that cock before you leave?" she asked, sitting on my lap.

I smiled. "Well, that just depends on how good your game plan sounds."

She licked her lips. "I'm gone show you why they call me Finnesse."

Chapter 17

J.T.

Boom! *Boom*! *Boom*! *Boom*! "Hell yeah, that muthafucka just crashed into a pole," Lil Momma hollered, hanging halfway out the window before sticking her head back in. She sat the gun on her lap, leaned over and kissed me on the cheek. "Fuck, I missed yo sexy ass."

"What about me?" Jennifer hollered from the back.

"I missed you too, Cuz. You know I was thinking about yo lil' yellow face all day, every day," she joked, and turned back to me.

I hit an ugly left and skirted on to a busy intersection with-the-sirens blaring and almost clipped another car. A broke up ass station wagon that looked like it was on its way out. Thank God the police had some good ass brakes, or we would have been in an accident.

"Oh my God, we gone die. Lawd Jesus, here I come. Please just let me come to heaven, 'cause we finna die!" Jamie wailed at the top of her lungs.

"Shut up!" the whole car said at one time, even Melanie.

Damn, she was annoying. I was already having a hard time concentrating, because there was so much shit going on around me. "We gotta get the fuck out of this car before they turn that helicopter loose," I said, pulling into a parking garage.

There was no way I was about to let us go out like that. This could not be our last chapter. I had to figure things out. We had to get out of this situation because I wanted to personally torture that nigga, Looney, and let my girls chop his ass up.

"Just let me out up there and I'll go get us another whip, J.T.," Lil Momma said with her door part of the way opened. I brought the car to a stop and she jumped out, after taking the gun and putting it into the small of her back. She ducked low to the ground, and wound up on the side of an all-black Lincoln Navigator 2018, newly released. I watched her break a corner of the window in the back, and then she was inside of the truck.

I parked the police car, and we cleaned as many of the weapons out of there as possible. As the girls were running to the truck, I was popping the trunk. It was loaded with bulletproof vests, flare guns, and an assault rifle, with multiple boxes of ammunition. I took all of that shit, and loaded it into our new vehicle.

Minutes later, we were pulling out with Lil Momma behind the wheel and me in the passenger's seat, looking the AR-33 over. An AR-33 was an assault rifle that spit rapidly. The magazine held thirty rounds, and every time you squeezed the trigger, it spit three bullets fast. I loved it because it gave you very little kick, and its accuracy was one hunnit.

"So, what we finna do now?" Jennifer asked, looking over her shoulders.

"Y'all can drop me off anywhere. I done had enough excitement for one day. I mean, I love you and all, J.T., but I ain't ready for all this. I need to get back in church. I miss Jesus so much. Lawd, I promise if you let me live through all of this, I'll be at church every Sunday. You all I need." She lowered her head and I could tell that she was serious.

"Are you kidding me? This has been the best day of my life. It's been one happening after the next. I feel like I'm in some sort of movie. I'm hoping we die at the end," Melanie said, with a crazy smile on her face.

The whole car was quiet for a long time. I mean, if there were any crickets around, you would have been able to hear them.

I wasn't planning on dying. Fuck that, we had a lot of shit to accomplish and we couldn't do none of it from the grave, so she was gone have to fall back with that theory. But, I was going to have my sister dropped off.

Lil Momma took a right and we wound up on the expressway flying. "I think we should get rid of her and Melanie, J.T. I mean, what purpose do either one of them serve now?"

"I don't wanna go nowhere. Please. Besides, the police are looking for me too. I didn't know that my room had cameras in them. They have all of what I did on tape. I'm screwed. Please don't abandon me now," she whimpered.

Jennifer sucked her teeth. "Hey Lil Momma, did you know that J.T. calls this bitch his Barbie?" She asked this question and mugged the shit out of Melanie.

Lil Momma shot daggers at me. "What do that mean? I hope you ain't develop no feelings for that bitch, because that ain't happening."

I shook my head. "Man, I knew her ever since she was two years old. She always been real pretty, and I used to call her my little Barbie. It's harmless. "

"Damn, so now its reeeaal pretty. I mean damn, so what does that make us?" Jennifer asked, turning red in the face.

"Well, did you know that while you were gone, Lil Momma, she fucked him?" Melanie spat, trying to shoot back at Jennifer.

Lil Momma gave me a look that said Melanie had better be lying. She looked at me so long that she almost smashed into the back of a semi-truck.

"Look out!" I hollered.

Errrrrr-uh! Vroommmmm! She slammed on the brakes and then at the last minute, swerved into the other lane, clipping a black Chevy Corsica, before stepping on the gas.

"I know this bitch better be lying, J.T. I know you didn't fuck my cousin while I was kidnapped somewhere. That don't sound like you to me."

"Baby, I was missing yo lil ass like crazy. We both were, and we just…"

"So, y'all fucked without me being there! What type of shit is that?" She blinked tears. "I didn't have no problem when it was all of us getting down. But, I never said it was okay for y'all to do that shit behind my back. That hurts so bad."

She shook her head from side to side.

"Lil Momma, I can explain," Jennifer began, then reached up to the driver's seat and touched her shoulder.

Lil Momma jerked away from her. "Don't touch me right now, Jennifer!"

"Y'all, please leave her alone before she crash into something. Ain't nobody trying to be dead on the highway. Everybody fucks everybody. That's why we all need to be in church. Lawd, know I'm gonna be there this Sunday. I'm sitting in the front row. Me and the preacher gone be looking each other right in the eye the whole time."

Lil Momma started to cry a little harder without saying anything for a long time. I reached over and put my hand on her thigh. "Baby, you know who I am. I love the fuck out of you, girl. Don't think because of what me and Jennifer did mean I don't love you, because I do."

She slowly shook her head and looked out onto the road. "So, I guess if I never came back, y'all would have been okay with that? If Looney would have killed me like he was planning on doing, y'all would have lived happily ever after. Huh?"

"Girl, you up there tripping. You know it ain't nothing like that. I already told you I ain't never fucking no other nigga but him, and you agreed with me. So, why you suddenly acting brand-new?" Jennifer asked, sounding annoyed.

Lil Momma stepped on the gas, and the truck shot forward.

"Because I'm hurt, bitch! That's why! Y'all wanted me dead? Okay then!" She switched to another lane and smashed into a small car, knocking it out of the way. It flipped over twice and landed in the gutter.

"Girl, slow yo ass down, what the fuck is wrong with you?" I hollered, ready to snatch her ass out of the driver's seat.

"Y'all want me to die? Okay. Let's all die then. Fuck this shit anyway!" She punched the truck to top speed and swerved into another lane, smacking a dude on a motorcycle. He flew off of his bike and wound up getting rolled over by a semi-truck.

"Lawd, Jesus take the wheel! Please take the wheel from this girl, because she gone kill us!" Jamie wailed. She started crying all loud and everything.

"Lil Momma, you know you overreacting right now. But, if you gone kill us then let's do it, because that's how it's supposed to go anyway. I'm supposed to die beside you. Not like this, but I'm gone let you pick our fate. So, if this is how you wanna go, knowing damn well that I love you, and your cousin love you, then let's do it."

"Yeah, we ride or die. I love you, girl, no matter what you think. You're my heart, and I'll die for you, or beside you any day." Tears sailed down her cheeks, as she reached and placed her hand on Lil Momma's shoulder.

Lil Momma stepped on the gas as tears continued to drip out of her eyes. Her head slightly lowered, and her eyes were slits. "I just love J.T. so much. I don't like him forgetting about me. I'm supposed to be his everything. I'm supposed to be the one that makes him do crazy things. The fact that his dick could even get hard while I was missing breaks my heart. I feel lost." She swerved into another lane and crashed into a Neon. Her airbag deployed. It looked like a little white balloon, and then the On-Star came on.

"On-Star, do you need any assistance?"

"Fuck assistance, bitch, we need Jesus. This bitch is going crazy!" Jamie hollered.

Lil Momma punched the gas again, and cars started blowing their horns all around us. I looked up ahead, and the highway was starting to veer to the left. It gave you only two options. You would have to slowly reduce your speed so you could venture off into the left lane that turned into a huge ramp, or you could keep on going straight and fly off of the bridge.

At the speed Lil Momma was going, it was going to be nearly impossible for her to make that lane adjustment. The way it was set up now, it looked as if we were going to fly off of the bridge and that had my heart beating fast. I didn't care about dying beside her, but I never envisioned it happening this way. I mean, I knew me and Jennifer was bogus because of what we had done. Lil Momma had always said she never minded us getting down, as long as she was there and a part of the equation in some way, which I understood.

A part of me felt like we betrayed her, and as a man I was willing to accept any outcome she felt would render her justice. I loved her, and to have hurt her was killing me

"Lil Momma, slow down please. Please slow down, oh my God, we about to die! We finna all be dead and resting in peace! Jesus, take the wheel from this girl. She crazy! Please!" Jamie cried with her mouth wide open.

The imperative turn was coming up faster and faster. I saw us going over the bridge and falling downward into the water beneath it. I knew I couldn't swim. I had never learned how to do that, which was crazy because in California it seemed like most people were born swimmers, but not me.

"Lil Momma, please don't do this. You know I love you. You're all I have in this world, besides J.T. You know I would never hurt you intentionally. Please think about it."

"Do it, Lil Momma! Do it! None of us have anything to live for anyway! Our lives are over," Melanie hollered. She sounded like she was excited. A pure adrenaline junkie.

"Bitch, shut up!" *Smack! Smack! Smack!* "I'm tired of yo shit. It's all your fault." *Smack! Smack! Smack!* Jennifer was out of her seat, whooping Melanie's ass. She had her pressed up against the window, smacking the shit out of her. "You wanna die so bad?"

"No! Ack! Accckk! Stop, ackk, it!" Now, Jennifer was choking her and banging her head against the window.

"Oh my God. Oh my God. They fighting and we about to die. Please, please! Puhleeeeze, Jesus, just save me. You can let them die, because they don't love you like I do. Lawd knows they don't. Save me, Father in Heaven."

We were about seventy-five yards away from the turn now. It was either going to happen or it wasn't. The closest car in our lane had already made the turn. I grabbed Lil Momma's thigh, and sat back in my seat. I felt like she had already made up her mind and I made peace with that.

Lil Momma started to shake her head. "I'm sorry, guys. I'm really, really sorry."

"Lil Momma! For God's sakes, you and I got down together too! So, you can't kill us because they made a mistake. We all been fucking! Don't do this! Don't take me away from my child! I am begging you!"

We were now fifty yards away from the turn. Jennifer reached over the seat, and squeezed Lil Momma's shoulder. "I love you, cousin. Please don't do this."

Lil Momma blinked back tears, and her feet slowly came off of the gas. She shook her head from left to right, and I noted snot dripping out of her nostril. She veered into the left lane and followed traffic the way she was supposed to. "You know what, I don't know what I'm going to do, but this isn't the way. I'll figure it out later, but this is not the way."

"Aww, man," Melanie said from the floor of the truck. Her nose was bleeding, and her hair all over the place.

Chapter 18

J.T.

It took two weeks before Finnesse could get everything set up the way it was supposed to be. She said it had taken so long because Vino had been out of town on business. His birthday had passed three days ago, but he still had his mind on celebrating his thirty-fourth year on earth.

So, there I was, sitting in a hotel room with Finnesse, trying to pick her brain and figure out the best way to get close enough to attack him. Vino had security. For as long as I had known him, he had always had some kind of protection around him, even in school. I always thought he was a coward that hid behind his family's money. The whole four years in school, I had never seen him stand toe to toe with any boy and fight for himself.

Instead, whenever it came down to that, he always had people to step in for him and do his dirty work. I couldn't respect a mafucka that couldn't handle their own business. To me, that was chump shit.

"Baby, are you listening to me?" Finnesse asked, grabbing my face and turning it slightly, so I was looking her in the eyes. I had zoned out for a second, finding different ways in to kill Vino when I was finally able to. "Yeah, that's my bad, baby. Tell me what's on your mind."

She smiled. "It's not what's on my mind, it's what has to be on yours, because you have to be focused in there tonight. Vino is going to have security all over the place. They watch him like a hawk." She stood up in front of me, looking down. "I know that we haven't known each other that long, but I still care about you, and I don't want to see anything happen to you. I can tell you are a really good man, and that you have a big heart. You still haven't told me why you want Vino so bad, but I'm sure you have a good enough reason."

I nodded. "Yeah, I do." I pulled her down so she was sitting on my lap. "Look, you ain't gotta worry about me. All you gotta do is stick to the script. When shit start getting freaky in there, you make sure you navigate around and take hold of as many of their guns as possible. After you feel like you've done as much as you can, you hit my phone and have the cellar door open, and I'll take shit from there. Just trust me."

"You have to remember it's going to be eight security guards there. He always has the same ones because he trusts them. I have done eleven parties now in honor of him and it is always the same guys. After a few drinks, everybody gets more relaxed and then the cocaine comes out. After that happens, the sex starts, and defenses are lowered. That's when I'll be able to strip some of the guys of their clothes, and weapons, and you can take it from there. Just remember, I want Aerial's ass done." She took a finger and slid it under her throat.

I nodded. "As soon as you hit my phone, just fall back and let me handle my business. In the meantime, I have somethin' else I gotta do."

* * *

I sat the bouquet of roses on Vonna's lap, leaned over and kissed her on the forehead, just as she was opening her eyes. As soon as she saw it was me, she smiled. "Hey beautiful, how are you doing?"

She licked her dry lips and tried to sit up in the bed and made a face like she was in pain. I hurried to help her, kissing her on the forehead afterward, and rubbing her soft cheek.

"I'm doing okay, Rip. I been worried about you, and missing Bree all at the same time. Have you heard anything about her?" She looked like she was on the verge of having a nervous breakdown.

I nodded. "Yeah, Lord willing we should have her back in the next day or so. I'm on top of it, you already know that. I miss her like crazy every single day." I blinked and a tear fell from my right eye.

She reached and wiped it away with her thumb. "I know, and she's a daddy's girl, so I know she's missing you more than she is me right now. But, that's okay. I still don't understand why you didn't allow for me to call the police. Don't you think they would have found her by now?" she asked, and then tried to sit up a little more, before reaching on the bed side table and grabbing her juice.

I ran my fingers through her hair while she sipped it. I was seeing my daughter's mother through new eyes. Every time she winced in pain, it was like I felt it and it made me want to break down. "Nall, because the person who has our daughter is well-connected. I don't trust the police to not tip him off. Besides, when have they ever cared about a black child?"

She lowered her head as the tears flowed down her cheeks. "I miss her so bad. I regret all of the times I made her cry. All of the times I told her to get away from me, or to go outside. I wish I could have them all back. I would do anything just to have her under me right now. I wish I knew if she was safe and sound. I wish I knew if they were feeding her? I miss our daughter, Rip, but I trust you, baby. I know you're going to get her back. Then, you'll take us away from all of this shit. We deserve better than this and you're the only one that can help us escape."

I was crying like a baby. I wasn't making no sounds or nothing, but I was on my knees with my face buried into her stomach, soaking the sheet wrapped around her in that hospital bed. I mean, all of it was coming out of me. All of the pain, the frustrations, the exhaustion, and the longing for Bree. The love a man has for his daughter is like no other.

It's like they are the most precious thing on earth, and they are all you see. They are delicate, and in need of constant protection, and when you fail as a man to protect your baby? Man, for me it was the worst feeling in the whole world, so I was having a hard time on keeping it together. I felt like I had failed my baby miserably.

Vonna rubbed my back. "I love you, baby and I believe in you. I know whoever has our baby, they are going to pay tenfold. I know how you get down. All I ask is that you be careful, Rip. Please, because if I lose you, if me and Bree lose you, we don't stand a chance in this world. You're all we have, and all that we need."

Those were all the words I needed to hear. I knew I had to do whatever it took to get my daughter back, and before it was all said and done, I would.

* * *

Lil Momma

"You wanna talk about this shit now, baby, instead of me and you walking around each other on eggshells?"

I looked over to J.T. as he closed the motel room door that connected to the room next to ours. I was seeing him through new eyes. I couldn't believe he could actually have sex with my cousin, while I was somewhere fighting for my life.

I just couldn't understand it and it was eating me up inside, to the point I was starting to feel sick and angry, all at once. "Yeah, let's talk about it, J.T., since you want to so fucking bad." I jumped up and got into his face. "How could you do me like that, huh? How could you fuck her without me being present, wasn't that the deal we agreed upon?"

He took a step back, and held me out at arms' length. "Look, baby, I know you mad, but you know you can't be all in my face like that. My temper is horrible."

I frowned, and turned my head slightly to the side, giving him a look that should have told him that I thought he had lost his fucking mind. "Oh, so now I'm supposed to be scared because you might lose your temper? How about you control yourself enough to explain to me, why you thought it was cool for you to break my heart? After all, I loved you with everything I had, J.T. I would have done anything for you, and this is how you do me after all we've been through." I sunk to my knees and broke down, crying my little heart out. I was really crushed, and I couldn't take it anymore.

I didn't have anybody left in my life that cared about me. J.T. and Jennifer was all that I had and I needed both of them equally, but differently. I was so lost, and so hurt all at once. All I could do was cry and cry harder.

J.T. sunk to his knees and wrapped his arms around me, hugging me tightly. I could hear him crying as well, and then I felt drips of water on my shoulder. "I'm so sorry, baby. I was stupid. I would have never hurt you like that, had I been in my right state of mind. You're my everything. I love you more than I love my own self and I would do anything for you, or about you. You're my life, and you always will be."

He squeezed me so tight, I could barely breathe. It was the first time I had ever heard him break down and it was scaring me, because he didn't cry.

As a female, I never wanted to see my man cry because seeing him in a state of weakness and vulnerability it made me feel ten times weaker. I looked to J.T. for guidance and strength and when I saw him panicking, or not knowing which way was up, or down, it caused me to freak all the way out horribly. So, while I was pissed at him for what him and Jennifer had done behind my back, I still needed him, and I didn't like seeing him in that state.

I returned his hug. "Baby, calm down, it's okay. I know you love me, and I love you back. I was just hurt, but everybody makes mistakes. Neither one of us are perfect but our bond is, and that's all we have to go off of. I forgive you one hundred percent. Do you hear me?"

In response, he gripped me tighter. I could feel his huge biceps swallowing me possessively. "I fucked up, baby, I'll never cross you like that again. I was just missing you, and she was missing you. Then shit just happened. It wasn't like we were doing it behind your back, as crazy as it may seem, but it was like you were there and by us connecting, we was in a sense bound by you. I mean, I don't know how to explain it, I just fucked up, and I wish I wouldn't have." He hugged me tighter.

I didn't know how to feel about what he had just said. I mean, had it come from any other man I would have never believed him for one second. But, this was J.T., a man I had been through it all with. I didn't feel like he would ever purposely hurt me. I felt things happened exactly the way he said they did. It was still killing me to imagine him and Jennifer rolling around in the bed together, moaning and groaning and I was nowhere to be found. I think that was the hardest part for me. It made me feel so jealous of her and worthless.

I hugged my man and rubbed his muscular back. "Baby, can you be honest with me?" I asked with my chin in the crook of his neck.

He backed up from me a little bit, and looked me in the eyes. His cheeks were still wet, and I could see him

170

searching my face in worry. "Yeah, baby, of course I will."

I cleared my throat. "When I was gone and you and Jennifer was doing y'all thing or whatever, did you at any point and time imagine yourself never seeing me again, and growing content with the fact that you still had her?"

He lowered his head for a second, then slowly shook it. "Damn. You know I have never lied to you ever since we have known each other."

Tears started to slide down my cheeks right away. My heart felt like it was somewhere in my chest, and I could barely breathe. I felt like I was bracing for somebody to hit me in the face with a baseball bat. "Yes, I know that J.T." I swallowed my spit. "And I don't expect you too right now either."

He looked up at me with watery eyes, blinked, and then tears ran down his cheeks, and I saw him swallow a few times. His Adam's apple moved up and down. "Baby, I didn't know if I was going to be able to find you because I know how that nigga, Looney, get down. Me and him grew up together and whenever we snatched something up, we always left it in a grave somewhere. So, I feared the worst for you, but that didn't mean I was gone ever stop looking for you."

I reached with both hands and wiped his tears away with my thumbs. "The truth, J.T." She exhaled loudly. "I imagined dude doing something fucked up to you, and me never seeing you again, and the only way I was able to maintain my sanity was honoring the fact that I would still have Jennifer. That if I never saw you again, at least I knew that she would hold me down, and be that ride or die chick like you was. She could never fill the void I would've had in me, but at least I wouldn't have straight out lost my mind. I would have still been able to fuck this city up over you, and have her to fall back on at the end if of the day."

I jumped up from the floor and ran in the bathroom purging my guts. I had never felt sicker in my whole entire life.

* * *

Jennifer

I was having a hard time hearing every word they were in there speaking, but I got the gist for the most part, and my heart was broken in two. How could J.T. make it seem like he didn't really care about me? Like I was just some mistake, he had slipped up and made. Any woman that felt the way I was feeling would have either snapped out or broke down crying. I chose to break down, because they were all that I had and me snapping out on them would have only made things worse.

I was pretty sure if it came down to him having to choose, he would have chosen her with no hesitation, and why wouldn't he? I was nothing. I was a nobody. I had to be kidding to think that he ever cared about me in the same light that I did him. So I was broken, and I was down to leave and let them do them.

I looked over my shoulder at Jamie and Melanie as they sat on the bed talking to each other, laughing like they didn't have a care in the world. I didn't understand it. I felt Looney was going to kill Jamie for betraying him, whenever he caught up to her. She also had a daughter I rarely ever heard her speak of. That was odd to me, but I guess to each their own.

Melanie's face was posted all over the news. She was wanted for murder, and they were probably scouring the country looking for her. She made it seem like she didn't even care. She said Jake had broken her heart so bad that she was ready to die, and I believed her. So yeah, maybe it was smart for me to just get away from everybody, but I had to talk to J.T. and Lil Momma first. There was no way around it.

Ten minutes later, Lil Momma was still in the bathroom with the water running, and I decided to stand in front of J.T., while he sat on the bed with his head down. "Look, J.T. I'm gone leave and let you and Lil Momma do y'all, because I'm clearly in the way, and I'm not trying to come in between what you two have."

He mugged me. "What? No the fuck you ain't. You ain't going nowhere. Now, I know some shit gotta be worked out, but at the end of the day, we're all family. Me, you, and her. Ain't nobody finna break that up. We just gotta get it together."

His response totally blew my wig back, because I was not expecting for him to come back at me like that. I thought he would have easily let me go. I didn't think I meant that much to him at all.

I blinked tears. "But, it's more than that, J.T., because I love you, even though I know I'm not supposed to. Then, on top of that, I'm pregnant."

His eyes got bucked and he looked at me for a long time, before falling onto his knees, pulling me down with him.

Chapter 19

Rip

"Okay, I just told one of his bodyguards to meet me in the pool house. He should already be there getting undressed. You let me do my thing with him for five minutes, and then you come in and handle your business. He's the only one that patrols the back of the house. You take him out, and we should be in the clear." She paused for a second. "Oh, and I'll make sure I leave the door open because I'm going in last."

That was seven minutes ago. I hopped the six-foot fence and fell directly onto my stomach, before low crawling across the grass in the night. The sky was full of stars. There was a light breeze out, and I could hear the sounds of Frank Sinatra coming from the house. Through the window, I could see people dancing, and seeming to have a good old time.

I pulled my mask down on my face and straightened my vest. The pool house was located right in the back of the mansion. I found it odd that it was isolated, and no one was out swimming. The pool even had its covering over the top of it. I figured Vino didn't want anybody dipping into his water. He was probably selfish like that, though I do remember him having some sort of germophobe when we were in high school, so maybe that could have been the case.

Anyway, I crawled alongside of the pool house until I got to a window. Once there, I peered inside and saw Finnesse laying down on the bed with a big and fat, Italian-looking man, taking his shirt off to reveal his hairy body. As soon as he was free of his shirt, he pulled off his shorts and got between her legs, she seemed to be reaching down to guide him inside of her. I nodded and

175

dropped to the ground, making my way around until I was at the door. I looked over my shoulder to make sure nobody was following me or watching me and as far as I knew, they weren't. It looked like the party was going off without a glitch in the distance.

I turned the knob and the door slowly opened. I pushed it in just enough for me to crawl inside. After I got in, I closed it back just as the sounds of lovemaking began on the bed.

"Umm, Finnesse, I been waiting all day for this. There is nothing like some good black pussy. God, it's the best," he grunted, moving in and out of her with short strokes.

I crept up to him as far as I could get, took the long wire out of my pocket and wrapped it around my hands a little bit, then jumped up and wrapped the excess three times around his neck and fell to the ground with his back to my chest.

"Ack! Ack! Ack! I. Ack! Can't." He slapped at my arm and tried to get me to turn him loose, but that only made me pull the wire harder. I was squeezing so hard, my hands were going numb. Saliva dripped out of the corner of my mouth as he continued to struggle under me.

Finnesse jumped up and looked down at him smiling. "Yes. Yes. Kill that son of a bitch. I hate him so much for all he's ever made me do. I want him dead. Dead." She clapped her hands together and jumped up and down.

"Chill, shorty, and get the fuck out of here. Go to the next spot so I can get in that house."

She nodded and on her way out, she stomped him in the chest just as I felt his struggles stop.

After I bodied him, I rolled him under the bed, and after getting off of my phone with Finnesse, I met her at the back door of the mansion. She stepped aside. "If you hurry up and go to the top of the stairs, you'll see a bathroom. It's the second door on your left. Paulie's in there. He's a big son of a bitch, so be careful. He's the guard that walks around the perimeter. The party is going on in front of the house. They're getting ready to sing Vino Happy Birthday, so hurry up. The timing is perfect."

I slipped past her and looked around as soon as I got into the house. I couldn't see anybody or anything. I could hear music off in the distance, and it smelled like cinnamon for some reason all around.

"Go to your left and up the stairs before he finishes. Hurry."

I flew up those stairs with murder on my mind. I felt if I could get rid of this bodyguard, then it would be that much easier to get to Vino. I knew for a fact I was gone torture that mafucka for even taking my daughter away from me. I didn't know where he was keeping her and there was nobody in his organization I felt I could go to and find out. My only hope was to torture the information out of him, and hope that I found my baby girl in time.

As soon as I made it to the top of the stairs, I looked down the long hallway and noted every door was closed. The hallway was lit up, and there were a few paintings on each side of the walls. I could tell they were expensive. I counted the doors on my left and noted there were only three of them, so the second one was easy to locate. I put a little pep in my step, going from one door to the next, placing my ear to them to try and see if I could hear anybody or anything unusual on the other side of them. After I confirmed that I did not, I went back in front of the door that Finnesse had directed me to.

Taking out my .40 Glock with the silencer, I slowly turned the knob and held my breath. As soon as I saw his big ass I was gone give him all face shots. I wanted to knock his brains out the back of his skull, and leave them dripping off of the shower curtain.

I took a deep breath and opened the door wide with my pistol raised, ready to buss, but what I saw was enough to give me a heart attack. I blinked tears right away and dropped my gun, before running inside of the bathroom.

There was Vonna, hanging from the pole that held the shower curtain. Her throat was not only slit, but it looked like somebody had cut into the same incision over and over again, so much so her head was barely hanging on, if not for the thick piece of skin that stopped it from coming completely off.

There was so much blood on the floor that it looked like a couple cans of burgundy paint had been spilled. Both of her wrists were slit, and they had carved out her eyes. On her forehead was the name, "Kelly." I ran into the bathroom and tried to get her down, with tears sailing down my cheeks.

I had failed to protect her. I felt so weak. I felt less there than dirt. I wish I could have traded my life for hers. Our entire childhood flashed through my mind. All of the years before I got into the game, where we were safe and sound. Just boyfriend and girlfriend, going to school, and our only worries were of what the other kids at school thought about us, one way or the other.

I was unwrapping the cord from around her neck when I heard, "Ahhhh! Help me!"

I took Vonna down and carried her into the hallway after kissing her over and over again on her forehead. I loved her so much. She really was a good woman. Stomp down for me, and always putting our daughter first, even though nobody ever taught her how to do that. I laid her on the floor, and whispered to her that she was my everything. I kissed her again, and picked up my gun. I felt that if they would do Vonna like this, then my daughter had to already have been dead. I was ready to go kamikaze.

"Hey, Rip! Get the fuck down here or this bitch is dead!" I recognized the voice of Vino.

I knelt down and kissed Vonna one more time. I was ready to die. I was ready to give these muthafuckas what they really wanted. I took my other .40 out the small of my back and cocked it. Double-breasted, I made my way to the stairs and looked down them, if the sight of Vonna had caused me to nearly have a heart attack, then what I saw now would surely kill me.

* * *

Lil Momma

"But, we gone definitely talk about this when I get back. Y'all just hang tight until then and nobody overreacts. I feel like we're family, we can handle this shit together. Do you understand?" J.T. said, looking specifically at me.

I nodded my head. "J.T., I already said I was cool with it. It just took me a little time to wrap my head around everything and now that I have, I'm telling you I'm okay. When you leave, me and my cousin gone get an understanding, and we'll go from there. This baby will be a part of all of us," I said, walking over to him and taking the pizza out of his hand. The box was still hot, and I was super hungry. "Where are you going anyway?

He leaned down and kissed me on the forehead. "I'm 'bout to go and meet with this nigga, Looney. I got some shit up my sleeve that's gone fuck homeboy over. I perfected it over the last few days and I can't lose. I'm gone keep my word and try not to harm Melanie, but I

179

promise the both of you on my life, by the end of the day, this nigga will be dead."

For as long as I had known him, J.T. had never made a promise he did not keep. For him to be saying he promised Looney would be dead by the end of the day, meant it was going to happen. I felt some type of way about watching him leave out of the hotel without me, but I had to stay back and get an understanding with Jennifer. She was pregnant with J.T.'s baby and we had to figure out what we were going to do. So, I kissed J.T. on the lips, and told him to be careful.

He and Melanie left out of the door with his arm around her. I knew it was more to hide their identities more than anything, but I still felt a twinge of jealousy. I closed the door and took a deep breath, before locking it. I noted Jamie was still asleep on the bed in the other connected room. I smiled and took the pizza and sat it on the blanket we had placed on the floor. For some reason, whenever me and Jennifer had sleepovers when we were little, we always ate pizza on the floor and had our little girl talk. So, I felt that even though we were older, it should have been no different.

She came and knelt down, as I sat the pizza on the floor in between us. She leaned over the box, grabbed my head and kissed me on the lips, smacking them loudly. After she pulled back, she brushed my hair out of my face. "Are you okay, girl?" Her voice was barely above a whisper, soothing, and gentle.

I really didn't know how I felt. I guess I was still hurt and a little angry, but I thought it wouldn't have been cool to keep up the drama. I had other things on my mind. I didn't want to be beefing with my cousin, so I lied. "Yeah, I honestly really am."

She smiled warmly. "I just want you to know that I love you, and that I would never intentionally hurt you. You're my world. You always have been." She reached over the pizza and kissed me again on the lips. This time, her kiss lingered and she ran her fingers through my hair. I melted. A part of me forgave her in that instant and I just wanted it to all be behind us. My love for J.T. was just so crazy though. So, every time I tried to mentally and emotionally move past the situation, I thought about them being together behind my back, and I felt sick on the stomach.

"Dang, y'all in here eating pizza? Why ain't nobody wake me up?" Jamie said, looking down on us from the doorway. Her hair was all over the place and she looked rough.

"Girl, you good, you better come over here and eat. We was just about to get ready and pray." My appetite was leaving all over again and I was starting to feel emotionally sick. I imagined J.T.'s baby growing inside of Jennifer and I wanted to throw up. I knew I had to put something on my stomach, so I figured I'd just eat half of a slice. I grabbed the knife, so I could cut me one of those bad boys in half.

Jamie came over and knelt down, reaching for Jennifer's hand. She took it and we all closed our eyes as Jennifer began to pray over our food. It was something she had always done ever since we were kids.

"Lord Jesus, we thank you for this meal. We pray that you please bless it and protect us from any impurities. Thank you for providing, Father, in Your Holy and Precious name we pray, A-Accccck! Helppp-acckkk! Accck! Acck! Nooo!"

"Ahhhhhh! Lil Momma! What are you doing?" Jamie screamed.

I had taken the knife and slammed it into my cousin's throat.

I used so much force that I saw the point of the blade poke out the back of her neck, before I yanked it out and slammed it into her again and again. She fell on her back holding her throat. I took the knife and slammed it into her face again and again. Her blood shot into my face. My blood, because she was my cousin, my flesh. More stabbing ensued. Jamie continued to scream behind me. I saw her fucking J.T. in my mind's eye. Saw her riding his dick and moaning, kissing all over his juicy lips, trying to make him forget about me. More stabbing, all in the face. I loved her so much. I grew up looking up to her.

She was my rock. She was always there when I needed her. I couldn't recall one time when she was not. Now, I was slashing the knife from side to side, making a mess like a preschooler in arts and crafts class. Her blood painted my face, then I was back to stabbing, hitting the bone in her face before the cloud faded from around me.

I looked down at her and she was unrecognizable. Her face was mangled, ruined. I flipped around and stabbed the knife downward into her stomach and pulled upward, making sure that the baby could never be born. J.T. was mine.

Jamie stopped screaming and jumped up from the floor, getting ready to run past me, until I stabbed her in the side and then in her thigh. She fell, and groaned. "No! Lil Momma, please don't do this to me," she begged.

I pushed her onto her stomach and straddled her back, raising the knife over my head, ready to bring it down, when the front door opened and J.T. came through it. As soon as he saw what was taking place, his eyes got big and he pulled out his .9 millimeter, aiming it at me as I brought the knife down with all of my might.

Boom! Boom! Boom!

I heard the shots even as the bullets ripped through my chest and blood splattered out of me. I toppled over onto my side. *Neither one of us won*, I thought, as the life seeped out of my body and death claimed me.

THE END

Submission Guidelines:

Submit the first three chapters of your completed manuscript to ldpsubmissions@gmail.com, subject line: Your book's title. The manuscript must be in a .doc file and sent as an attachment. Document should be in Times New Roman, double spaced and in size 12 font. Also, provide your synopsis and full contact information. If sending multiple submissions, they must each be in a separate email.

Have a story but no way to send it electronically? You can still submit to LDP/Ca$h Presents. Send in the first three chapters, written or typed, of your completed manuscript to:

LDP: Submissions Dept
Po Box 870494
Mesquite, Tx 75187

DO NOT send original manuscript. Must be a duplicate.

Provide your synopsis and a cover letter containing your full contact information.

Thanks for considering LDP and Ca$h Presents.

Coming Soon from Lock Down Publications/Ca$h Presents

BOW DOWN TO MY GANGSTA

By **Ca$h**

TORN BETWEEN TWO

By **Coffee**

BLOOD STAINS OF A SHOTTA **III**

By **Jamaica**

WHEN THE STREETS CLAP BACK **III**

By **Jibril Williams**

STEADY MOBBIN

By **Marcellus Allen**

BLOOD OF A BOSS **V**

By **Askari**

LOYAL TO THE GAME **IV**

By **T.J. & Jelissa**

A DOPEBOY'S PRAYER **II**

By **Eddie "Wolf" Lee**

IF LOVING YOU IS WRONG... **III**

LOVE ME EVEN WHEN IT HURTS

By **Jelissa**

TRAPHOUSE KING **II**

By **Hood Rich**

BLAST FOR ME **II**

RAISED AS A GOON **V**

Blast For Me 2

By **Ghost**

ADDICTIED TO THE DRAMA **III**

By **Jamila Mathis**

LIPSTICK KILLAH **III**

By **Mimi**

WHAT BAD BITCHES DO **III**

By **Aryanna**

THE COST OF LOYALTY **II**

By **Kweli**

SHE FELL IN LOVE WITH A REAL ONE

By **Tamara Butler**

LOVE SHOULDN'T HURT II

By **Meesha**

CORRUPTED BY A GANGSTA **II**

By **Destiny Skai**

SHE FELL IN LOVE WITH A REAL ONE II

By **Tamara Butler**

A GANGSTER'S CODE II

By **J-Blunt**

TRUE SAVAGE 5

By **Chris Green**

KING OF NEW YORK

By **TJ EDWARDS**

CRIME OF PASSION

By **MiMi**

Ghost
CUM FOR ME 4
LDP Compilation

Available Now

<u>RESTRAINING ORDER</u> **I & II**
By **CA$H & Coffee**
<u>LOVE KNOWS NO BOUNDARIES</u> **I II & III**
By **Coffee**
<u>RAISED AS A GOON I, II, III & IV</u>
<u>BRED BY THE SLUMS I, II, III</u>
<u>BLAST FOR ME</u>
By **Ghost**
<u>LAY IT DOWN</u> **I & II**
<u>LAST OF A DYING BREED</u>
<u>BLOOD STAINS OF A SHOTTA I & II</u>
By **Jamaica**
<u>LOYAL TO THE GAME</u>
<u>LOYAL TO THE GAME II</u>
<u>LOYAL TO THE GAME III</u>
By **TJ & Jelissa**
<u>BLOODY COMMAS I, II & III</u>
<u>SKI MASK CARTEL I & II</u>
By **T.J. Edwards**
<u>IF LOVING HIM IS WRONG…I & II</u>
By **Jelissa**
<u>WHEN THE STREETS CLAP BACK I & II</u>
By **Jibril Williams**
<u>A DISTINGUISHED THUG STOLE MY HEART</u>
<u>I II & III</u>
<u>LOVE SHOULDN'T HURT</u>
By **Meesha**

Ghost
A GANGSTER'S CODE
By **J-Blunt**
PUSH IT TO THE LIMIT
By **Bre' Hayes**
BLOOD OF A BOSS **I, II, III & IV**
By **Askari**
THE STREETS BLEED MURDER **I, II & III**
THE HEART OF A GANGSTA I II& III
By **Jerry Jackson**
CUM FOR ME
CUM FOR ME 2
CUM FOR ME 3
An LDP Erotica Collaboration
BRIDE OF A HUSTLA **I II & II**
THE FETTI GIRLS **I, II& III**
CORRUPTED BY A GANGSTA
By **Destiny Skai**
WHEN A GOOD GIRL GOES BAD
By **Adrienne**
A GANGSTER'S REVENGE **I II III & IV**
THE BOSS MAN'S DAUGHTERS
THE BOSS MAN'S DAUGHTERS II
THE BOSSMAN'S DAUGHTERS III
THE BOSSMAN'S DAUGHTERS IV
A SAVAGE LOVE **I & II**
BAE BELONGS TO ME
A HUSTLER'S DECEIT I, II
WHAT BAD BITCHES DO I, II
By **Aryanna**
A KINGPIN'S AMBITON

Blast For Me 2

A KINGPIN'S AMBITION **II**

I MURDER FOR THE DOUGH

By **Ambitious**

TRUE SAVAGE

TRUE SAVAGE II

TRUE SAVAGE **III**

TRUE SAVAGE **IV**

By **Chris Green**

A DOPEBOY'S PRAYER

By **Eddie "Wolf" Lee**

THE KING CARTEL **I, II & III**

By **Frank Gresham**

THESE NIGGAS AIN'T LOYAL **I, II & III**

By **Nikki Tee**

GANGSTA SHYT **I II &III**

By **CATO**

THE ULTIMATE BETRAYAL

By **Phoenix**

Boss'n Up I, II & III

By **Royal Nicole**

I LOVE YOU TO DEATH

By **Destiny J**

I RIDE FOR MY HITTA

I STILL RIDE FOR MY HITTA

By **Misty Holt**

LOVE & CHASIN' PAPER

By **Qay Crockett**

TO DIE IN VAIN

By **ASAD**

Ghost
BROOKLYN HUSTLAZ
By **Boogsy Morina**
BROOKLYN ON LOCK I & II
By **Sonovia**
GANGSTA CITY
By **Teddy Duke**
A DRUG KING AND HIS DIAMOND I & II
A DOPEMAN'S RICHES
By **Nicole Goosby**
TRAPHOUSE KING
By **Hood Rich**
LIPSTICK KILLAH **I, II**
By **Mimi**
A GANGSTER'S CODE
By **J-Blunt**
WHO SHOT YA
By **Renta**
SHE FELL IN LOVE WITH A REAL
By **Tamara Butler**

BOOKS BY LDP'S CEO, CA$H

TRUST IN NO MAN

TRUST IN NO MAN 2

TRUST IN NO MAN 3

BONDED BY BLOOD

SHORTY GOT A THUG

THUGS CRY

THUGS CRY 2

THUGS CRY 3

TRUST NO BITCH

TRUST NO BITCH 2

TRUST NO BITCH 3

TIL MY CASKET DROPS

RESTRAINING ORDER

RESTRAINING ORDER 2

IN LOVE WITH A CONVICT

Coming Soon

BONDED BY BLOOD 2

BOW DOWN TO MY GANGSTA